HERE, KITTY, KITTY . . .

"Hello. Mrs. Walker. Anyone home?"

There was no response. I stepped into the hall. I was well aware that I was trespassing, but figured that my priority was to find Mavis's cat. . . .

I moved forward cautiously. "Mrs. Walker," I whispered.

No answer. I knelt down beside her. "Mrs. Walker? Lizzie? Wake up."

Gently I pushed on her shoulder to turn her over. Her eyes were wide open, as if in terror. Even before I fumbled for the pulse on her neck, I knew it was futile. Feeling something damp and sticky on my fingers, I recoiled in horror as I realized that blood had seeped from a wound on the back of her head. . . . I ran down the hall, flung open the front door, and practically fell into the arms of the man standing there.

Detective Jack Mallory was the first to recover.

"Mrs. Doolittle?" He raised shaggy grey eyebrows in surprise. "Where are you going in such a hurry?"

Delilah Doolittle AND THE Careless Coyote

Patricia Guiver

BERKLEY PRIME CRIME, NEW YORK

DELILAH DOOLITTLE AND THE CARELESS COYOTE

A Berkley Prime Crime Book / published by arrangement with the author

PRINTING HISTORY
Berkley Prime Crime edition / November 1998

For information address: The Berkley Publishing Group, a member of Penguin Putnam Inc., 375 Hudson Street, New York, New York 10014.

The Penguin Putnam World Wide Web site address is http://www.penguinputnam.com

ISBN: 0-425-16612-0

Berkley Prime Crime Books are published by The Berkley Publishing Group, a member of Penguin Putnam Inc., 375 Hudson Street, New York, New York 10014.

PRINTED IN THE UNITED STATES OF AMERICA

10 9 8 7 6 5 4 3 2 1

For Lizzie

and

For my moggies Darcy, Natasha and Misty, shelter alumni all, who daily direct the work flow. They rearrange papers, paw at the words appearing on the screen, and, when all else fails, will sit on the keyboard to remind me it's dinnertime.

Acknowledgments

Thanks to Karin Christensen who taught me the ways of the ferals; and to feral cat feeders everywhere whose compassion for and dedication to the unfortunate cats left to fend for themselves—in parks, abandoned buildings, and vacated apartments—have my utmost admiration.

"When all candles be out, all cats be gray."

JOHN HEYWOOD, *PROVERBS* (1546)

Delilah Doolittle
AND THE
Careless Coyote

1

The Dispossessed

"NO, WATSON! STAY away from there! There's a cat inside. You'll get your nose scratched," I warned my big red Doberman as I shoved aside pet carriers, catch-poles, old towels, and blankets—tools of the pet detective's trade—to make room in the back of my old Ford station wagon for the heavy cat trap.

"Come and sit up front and keep me company," I told her, transferring a cardboard box containing leashes, packets of jerky treats, tins of sardines and tuna, and a snakebite kit, from the front seat to the back, wedging it against the trap to prevent it from shifting once we set off for the vet.

My voice expressed the uneasiness I'd been unable to shake ever since arriving before dawn at the cliffs above Dog Beach. I was anxious to get going before I had further close encounters with the dispossessed.

The coyote for one. If I hadn't been doing the Andersons a favour, I would never have seen him, lean and wary, slipping like a grey ghost through the early-morning mist, following the imprint of his ancestors, and before them, the prehistoric mammoths that walked these southern California hills ten thousand years ago. Eventually he would have picked up the bike trail that paralleled the flood-control channel from the inland canyons to the ocean, then crossed Pacific Coast Highway to reach the feral cat colony where I was surprised to find myself that early-autumn morning.

"We hate to ask you, Delilah, but we've already set the trap," Joan Anderson had said, going on to explain that she and husband, Bill, had set the humane trap the previous evening, only later getting the phone call about a family emergency out of town. "All you have to do is check it early, before daylight. If there's a cat, take it to Dr. Willie. We'll be home in a couple of days. Ta, love."

British transplants like myself, the Andersons were part of the loose network of animal lovers who monitored feral cat colonies nationwide—worldwide, in fact, I thought, recalling the "moggies" of the mossy woods in my native England. In most cases the ferals, usually the offspring of abandoned pets, were trapped, spayed or neutered, vaccinated, ear-notched, and released back to the colony.

A sign erected by Surf City's public-works department stating that it was unlawful to abandon animals apparently had little effect on those who regarded pets as a disposable commodity.

The Andersons had made this colony their life's work, dedicating their hearts and souls, not to mention a small fortune, to the cats no one else cared about. They knew them all by name, and household pets couldn't be better looked after. Except that the ferals were vulnerable to other wild creatures, particularly the coyote, now heading for the area where Joan and Bill had left out food the previous evening.

But coyotes were not the ferals' only enemy. Some people claimed that the cats were a health hazard and should be rounded up and euthanized. Bird lovers blamed them for declining songbird populations. Though others, myself included, considered that the real cause of that calamity might more appropriately be laid at the doors of deforestation, pesticides, and development.

Recently traps had been stolen or destroyed. But Joan and Bill remained steadfast to their cause. Morning and evening, whatever the weather, they were there to tend their flock. It would take an extreme emergency, in this case a death in the family, for them to abandon their post.

I couldn't refuse to help. If the cat took the bait, it would be helpless. Hidden in the bushes, the trap might go unnoticed for days.

Belly low to the ground, the coyote was now stalking a group of cats fighting over the remains of food left on paper plates along the cliff path. I picked up a stone and threw it in their general direction, to alert the cats and distract the coyote. I didn't want any feline assassinations on my watch.

As the stone hit the ground the cats scattered and the coyote vanished into the bushes to reconsider his strategy.

I located the metal cage-like trap, covered with a blanket, in the bushes just off the pathway. The gate was closed and I approached with caution. Maybe, instead of a cat, an opossum or a skunk, lured by the strong-smelling tuna bait, had stepped on the metal plate, tripping the mechanism. Donning protective leather gloves, I warily lifted one end of the blanket. I gasped. Instead of the scraggly old tiger I might have expected, a large sable Burmese stared out at me with panicky, deep gold eyes.

This must be somebody's pet! Surely no one would abandon such a beautiful animal. But then I recalled Joan telling me of other purebreds she had found here—Siamese, Persians, even a rare Ocicat.

Perhaps he was a stray. I would check my lost-and-found ads when I got home. Whatever the case, I was sure Joan and Bill would be able to find a new home for this beauty.

Glad that I'd had the foresight to wear my old jeans for this grubby job, I crouched down in the dirt and spoke softly to the cat.

"It's okay," I said, hoping my low, even tone would calm him. "Dr. Willie's going to take good care of you."

His only response was to hiss as I lifted the trap and started back up the cliff path.

At that hour I did not expect anyone else to be about, and was surprised to see a man walking somewhat aimlessly toward me. A homeless creature of a different sort, perhaps, up early to ease limbs stiff from a night of sleeping on the hard ground. Dressed in grey sweats, his feet bare, he was of medium build and height. His face was partly shrouded by the hood of his sweatshirt, but there was something vaguely familiar about him. I couldn't be sure in this light, and didn't wish to stare. I wondered if perhaps he was the one responsible for destroying the traps, and if so, seeing me carrying one, he might take it into his head to set about me, physically or verbally. He hugged something close to his chest. I couldn't make out what it was, but fearful that it might be a weapon, I stood aside to let him pass. I felt vulnerable, lumbered as I was with the trap, and wished Watson was with me. I'd had to leave her in the car; she would have scared the cats. But the man passed by, seemingly oblivious of my presence, and I continued on my way, the unwieldy trap bouncing wildly as its occupant grew more and more agitated.

As I reached the car, a sudden gust of wind caught at my hair, and brought with it the acrid smell of smoke drifting from the Cleveland National Forest, where a fire had been raging out of control for several days. It was October. Midday temperatures were pushing one hundred degrees, and after a rainless summer, the brush was tinder dry. All it took was a spark, fanned by the Santa Ana winds, to create a fierce brushfire.

"We're in for another scorcher," I told Watson as I drove the short distance along Pacific Coast Highway to the beachside cottage which served our veterinarian as both home and office.

The vet was in his front yard setting up a large

wooden pelican which had apparently blown over. In its beak the bird held a sign announcing WELLINGTON SCOTT, DVM. A red-and-green surfboard leaning against the side of the house still dripped seawater.

Dr. Willie, as he was known to his friends, had obviously only just returned from the beach. Clad in a purple wet suit, his long black hair, escaping from a usually neat ponytail, whipped around his face in the wind. He was in his mid-thirties, a good twenty years my junior, but I could still recognize a hunk when I saw one. At six-foot-plus, he was at least twelve inches taller than I. Stand too close and I could get a crick in my neck.

"How's the surf?" I asked.

"Waves are too choppy," he said. "Darn wind. Good weather for pet detectives, though," he added, a grin lighting his handsome olive-complexioned face.

He was right. I'd had more calls concerning lost dogs during the past three days than during the entire preceding month. When the Santa Anas blow, gates fly open, fences come down, and away the dogs go—whither they know not, and neither do they care—until they get hungry and tired. By the time their owners come home from work, their pets might be miles away. Most would be located at the animal shelter within a couple of days. But there were always exceptions, and I would be called in to hunt for the doggie MIAs.

Such was the case when a tree had crashed onto the garage roof of a local residence, and two Alaskan Malamutes, confined there while their owners were at work, had escaped. Because the dogs were wearing license tags, the Lindstroms had let several days pass, anticipating a call from animal control. But no call came, and finally they contacted me. After an initial search of local shelters, I had dispatched one of my BOLO ("Be on the Lookout") flyers to shelters in neighbouring counties on the chance that Matt and Matilda might have been picked up by someone who had then transported them farther afield.

I handed the carrier to Dr. Willie.

"Joan called and told me you might come by," he said.

"This one's lucky to have survived," I said, and told him about the coyote. "I was so surprised to see him. He had to negotiate a couple of freeways, not to mention get through town and across PCH to reach Dog Beach."

"It's the fires," he said. "As habitats are destroyed, and the small game disappears, a hungry coyote will go anywhere he can find food."

"Well, he seems to have scoped out the feral cat colony pretty well," I said.

Dr. Willie nodded. "You watch," he said as he walked me to my car. "He'll be picking off pets in backyards next. Ground squirrel, cat or poodle, it's all the same to a coyote."

I agreed. I didn't feel we could ascribe anything more sinister to the coyote than a desire to survive, just like the rest of us.

"People should keep their pets indoors," I muttered to Watson as we made our way home. "What's the point in having a dog or cat if you're just going to chuck it out in the backyard?''

Watson pressed closer to me on the wagon's bench seat as if to assure me she knew where she was well-off.

As I turned off PCH and drove along the palm-tree-lined half block past the forties- and fifties-vintage summer cottages to my home, I tsked in annoyance.

''Of all the bloody cheek!'' I said to Watson. ''Just look at that!''

A red Corvette stood in my driveway, leaving me nowhere to park.

2

The Lady in Red

My tiny two-bedroom home afforded only a single-car garage, and since the Corvette was in the driveway, I was obliged to park on the street. Fortunately, that early in the morning there was still space in front of my house. Later in the day I would be lucky if I could get in or out of my own driveway, as beachgoers parked wherever they could find meter-free space.

The cause of my current inconvenience was sitting in a deck chair on my front porch.

Mavis Byrde was a work of art, even at this hour. With very little makeup on flawless skin, she could get away with claiming to be ten years younger than she actually was—and she did. Fortunately for her, the weather was still warm, for the flimsy red negligee she was wearing, though covering the bare essentials, was not designed for warmth. Her wispy grey-blonde hair was caught in an up-do with a red ribbon. On her feet she wore tiny red mules with heels, those silly fluffy things rarely seen outside of a lingerie catalogue. An astonishing sight at any time of the day, at six o'clock in the morning, Mavis's appearance bordered on the bizarre.

I did not know her well, only that she was originally from the south—New Orleans, I think it was—that she taught piano, often performing at local charity events, and that her hobby was breeding and showing Abyssinian cats—sleek red- or ruddy-coated, green-eyed aristocrats that fetched large sums amongst the fancy. My personal cat ownership (stewardship might be the better word) was limited to Hobo, the hard-bitten, half-feral, three-legged ginger tom who occasionally condescended to seek refuge from the elements on my back porch, sometimes even accessing the kitchen through Watson's doggie door. It escapes me why anyone would feel compelled to bring more cats into a world already surfeited with same. To purchase one seems to me the height of extravagance, when any Laundromat bulletin board, community newspaper, and, alas, many a Dumpster, will provide more unwanted kittens than your average person could possibly desire.

Mavis Byrde was not your average person.

"Mavis. This is a surprise," I called as I let Watson out the rear door of the wagon. "What brings you here so early in the morning?"

She stood at my approach. "Delilah! Thank goodness you're back. I hope you don't mind me waiting. I just didn't know what else to do. I've been praying you weren't gone for the day. I'm just so distraught." Her voice, light, little girly, belied her age, which even the most generous, or nearsighted, would have to put at around fifty. She looked nervously at Watson.

Seeing her apprehension, I kept the Dobie at my side with a "Stay," as, naturally enough, she had been about to bound up to the front door.

"She's harmless. A pussycat," I assured my visitor.

At the word *pussycat,* Mavis sat back down suddenly. Her face crumpled, and I thought she was about to cry.

"I say. Are you all right? What's the problem? Really, she's the sweetest, gentlest dog. See?" Holding Watson close to my side with her collar, I once again attempted to climb the steps to the porch.

"No, you don't understand," she cried. "The police refuse to help, even though I told them Meowzart was valuable property. They said it's not their job, and referred me to the animal shelter. But I looked and looked, and he's not there. They told me to call you."

"You've lost your cat?" I broke in.

"Yes," she said, and after continuing her litany of false starts and dead ends, finally got out. "I called Estelle LaBelle, the pet psychic. She's supposed to be very good. Fifty dollars for a ten-minute telephone reading, she charges. But all she could tell me was that she could see Meowzart in a dark place. Oh dear. He must be so frightened. Please, Delilah. You're my only hope."

No one likes to think of herself as a last resort, particularly coming after a pet psychic who, stretching credulity to the limit, claimed to be able to trace missing pets without leaving the house. Dark place, indeed! However, I did my best to look concerned.

Mavis went on. "I couldn't sleep all night. I was out

looking for him again early this morning, all up and down the street, before I got dressed.'' Glancing down at her getup, she giggled nervously.

Early-morning joggers and surfers on their way to the beach were beginning to stare. I don't usually hold business consultations on my front porch, let alone with people in their night attire.

''Well, if you've lost a pet, I might be able to help,'' I said, trying to follow the rambling narrative of her search for her lost cat. ''Let's go inside, and you can tell me more about it.''

I led the way through the small entryway into the kitchen, conscious of the untidy state in which I had left the place in my dash out of the house earlier.

I was not in the best of moods, having had to leave without my customary three cups of tea. I'd forgotten to set the alarm, and had practically fallen out of bed and into my clothes in my haste to get to the cat colony before daylight. In fact, for all the inappropriateness of her outfit, I rather thought that Mavis was the better turned out of the two of us. In old jeans covered in cat hair, and torn tennies, I was no match for her.

I plugged in the electric kettle. ''Would you like a cup of tea?'' I asked.

Mavis nodded yes. Better not put too much tea in the pot, I thought. She didn't look the type who would enjoy the strong English brew, diluted with milk and heavy on the sugar, that my ex-pat Brit friends preferred.

Watson climbed onto her old armchair, the leather worn and scratched by her heavy claws, her expression one of concerned anticipation of the conversation that was to follow.

"Now tell me how I can help you," I said.

Meowzart, Mavis's prize stud male Abyssinian, had disappeared. "I can't understand it," she said. "My cats never go outside. I don't allow it. Too dangerous."

Here we were in agreement. If I had my way, all cats would be kept indoors by law. The hazards for the outdoor cat are many, in particular the four *C*s familiar to all cat rescuers—other cats, cars, coyotes, and worst of all, creeps.

Mavis pushed her long blonde fringe out of her eyes and continued. "Though Meowzart, more than Pussini and Depussy, is always looking for an opportunity. He's fascinated by the birds and butterflies he sees through the window." She smiled wanly. As soon as she realized he'd gone, she had started to look for him, and could swear she saw him in her neighbour Lizzie Walker's backyard. "A disgrace, that yard of hers is," she said in disgust. She had knocked on Lizzie's door to ask if she might search the yard, but the "crazy old woman wouldn't even open the door. I knocked and shouted for half an hour. After that, I called the police."

I'm rather afraid that cat stealing ranks very low on the police priority list, supposing it appears there at all. So now Mavis had turned to me for help.

I took my time thinking about it, busying myself with the tea tray, checking my guest's teacup, barely touched.

I already had a full caseload, and I really don't like taking cat cases.

Cats are hard to find, harder still to catch once you've found them, and since their owners seldom report them missing immediately, the trail gets cold. A pet detective, like any other, relies on people's recollections, and while they will usually remember seeing a stray dog, a stray cat seldom impinges on their memory. No idle barking, no dodging traffic, no following children home from school. Waggy-tailed friendly, or surly and menacing, whatever its disposition, one knows when there's a stray dog around. But cats are unobtrusive in their lostness. They make no fuss, no noise. They climb and hide in unlikely places. If they get sick, they creep away to die. Often cat owners are not even aware their pet is missing until it's been gone several days. "He'll come home when he's hungry," is the usual attitude. Thousands of cats are put to sleep every year because it never occurs to their owners to check the shelters.

Mavis seemed to sense my hesitation.

"Please help me find him," she said. "Meowzart is very valuable. And I'm offering a reward. I'm prepared to take money that I had set aside in my will to send my cats to the Buttercup Cat Retirement Home should anything happen to me." Tears welled up in her pale blue eyes. "I'm so frightened, with all these cat murders lately," she added.

"Whatever do you mean?"

"You haven't heard?" Her delicate eyebrows shot up in surprise. "It was on the eleven o'clock news last night. Cats are being found dead all over the neighbourhood. There's talk that they're being used in some kind of ritual sacrifice.'' Mavis's eyes narrowed. ''I think Lizzie Walker might be involved. I'm sure she's got my cat. There's something strange going on in that house. Why wouldn't she open the door to me? She might even be a witch! You've got to help me.''

This was indeed news to me. I had gone to bed early the previous evening, in preparation for my pre-dawn visit to the cat colony, and had missed the late-night news broadcast.

I was no more prepared, however, to believe that poor old Lizzie Walker, a local cat collector, was a witch than I was ready to accept that cultists were responsible for the rash of cat deaths. There had to be a more plausible explanation. Lizzie was eccentric, yes, but quite harmless. It was possible that she had added Meowzart to her collection. If so, it shouldn't be too difficult to talk her out of him, especially if a reward was offered.

Feeling sure that I could retrieve Meowzart with very little inconvenience, I proceeded to inform Mavis of my terms: seventy-five dollars a day, plus expenses (for flyers, classified ads) and a hundred-dollars nonrefundable deposit.

She readily agreed, and I reached for my pad and pen to take down the information I needed. Her address, on Walnut Avenue in the Parkside district of town, phone number, a description of the cat—intact male, red, short-haired, green eyes—though one red Abyssinian cat would look pretty much like another to me, and I doubted if there was more than one at large in Surf City on any given day.

"Last seen?"

"He must have slipped out early yesterday morning, when I went to get the newspaper. I remember the wind blowing the door wide open after I thought I'd closed it. I'm always so careful about doors," she added.

"Any ID?"

"No. He never gets out." Then, realizing the absurdity of that statement, she added apologetically, "I think collars are unsafe on cats."

I could have pointed out that pet stores carry a wide selection of breakaway collars, especially designed to prevent a cat from becoming entangled in a bush or a tree. But I decided to save that piece of advice for later, when I was able to return the cat.

I stood at the front door and watched as Mavis made her way down the pathway, stepping carefully to avoid catching her high heels between the paving stones. She turned to wave as, with enviable elegance, she lowered her red chiffon-clad self into the Corvette's bucket seat.

I returned to the kitchen, poured myself another cup of tea, and sat down to read the still-folded *Los Angeles Times*. The headline leaped at me from the bottom of the front page:

CAT KILLINGS SPARK DEMAND FOR ACTION

At an emotional meeting last night, residents of the Parkside neighborhood in Surf City demanded that local officials mount an aggressive investigation into the recent killings of cats that have been occurring in the area. Residents report that they are living in a climate of fear as a result of the recent animal deaths. . . .

Mike Denver, Surf City's chief animal control officer, who I had known since his entry-level days as a kennel attendant, was quoted as saying he believed that the killings were the work of coyotes, but promised a full investigation and report by the next meeting.

I thought of Hobo, out on the wetlands. Too cagey by half, even on three legs, to be caught by any predator, four-legged or two-legged, I reassured myself. But as I read on, my tea getting cold, an unpleasant prickling sensation down the back of my neck warned me that my new case might involve something a bit more sinister than a simple case of a runaway cat.

3

Lizzie the Cat Lady

ON THE CHANCE that somebody had found Meowzart and had placed an ad in the lost-and-found column, I turned to the classified section. Nothing resembling an Abyssinian was listed, and I was surprised to find that there were more losts than founds. Usually it's the other way around, leading one to the dismaying conclusion that many owners don't care enough to go looking for their pets. Even more surprising was that most of the lost cats were local. What was happening to the cats of Surf City? Well, I was determined to locate at least one of them. Time to go looking for Meowzart.

I put the paper aside and got ready to restart my day. I was feeling decidedly grotty after my early-morning sojourn in the bushes at the cat colony, but after a shower and a change of clothing, I was refreshed and ready to tackle Lizzie Walker. I slathered SPF-thirty sunblock on my fair English skin. The combination of sun and wind could result in a bad burn, even this late in the year. I put on a pair of cotton khaki slacks, a brown-and-white-checked shirt, and a tan sport cap to keep my hair in place in the wind and, not incidentally, to cover the grey streaks among the chestnut. It was time for another tint. That was the trouble: once started it had to be kept up. I had my friend Evie to thank for that. She was forever goading me to do "something" about my hair. It was no use arguing with her. She was one of those people who had an answer for everything. As she was quick to point out, she only wanted the best for me, and the best, in her opinion, was a Really Nice Man. One had to be prepared at all times in case one of these paragons, of whom she had what appeared to be an endless supply, should make an appearance. Whenever I visited her at her home in San Diego, she would trot out a new RNM—usually a business acquaintance of her husband, Howard's—quite presentable, and decent company for an evening. But she had yet to introduce me to anyone in whom I could summon up more than a passing interest. My brief marriage to Roger, exciting and wonderful as it had been until his untimely death a few years earlier, had left me not only shattered, but with both a very high standard of what I expected in a spouse and a doubt that I was marriage material. I enjoyed my independence too much. More importantly, where would I find someone with the same interests—in animals, photography, the environment—not to mention a high tolerance for dog hair on the furniture? Love me, love my dog, was my motto.

By the time I was ready to leave, the wind had picked up in earnest. Through the window I could see the trees swaying wildly. How did the birds cope? I wondered, picturing them clinging to branches for dear life as the trees tried to shake them loose.

Watson, watching my every move, was on her feet as soon as I picked up the car keys.

"We'll need rocks in our pockets to keep our feet on the ground today, old girl," I said to her. At seven and a half stone I was only a few pounds heavier than she, a condition that could be a blessing (as when I had to crawl through the doggie door the day I locked my keys in the car) or a curse (being invisible to all but the most attentive of salesclerks). My height, or lack of it, added to the problem. At five-one, I was afflicted with what my father used to call duck's disease—as in walking with one's behind too close to the ground.

By the time I was ready to face the world, the post had been delivered, and I stopped to check the mailbox at the end of the driveway.

Another quaint American custom, that. In England the mail is dropped through a letter box into the hall. Much more secure. Not that security was of much concern with my mail. It was mostly junk, anyway. Distressing to think how many trees gave their lives to satisfy this amazing penchant for direct-mail advertising, much of it unsolicited and unwelcome, often addressed simply to *Resident*. Why in heaven's name did they write to me if they didn't even know my name? On top of today's batch was an offensive flyer from a company named Meet Your Match. I had no desire to be matched with someone who was as likely as I no doubt would be to lie on the application, supposing I was in the least inclined to respond. This was followed by an invitation to join the American Association of Retired Persons. Really, if they knew how unwelcome such reminders of advancing years were, they would try a different recruitment strategy. I'm fifty-fivish and plan to remain so for as long as I can get away with it.

Only two pieces of personal mail: a postcard from Dr. Willie reminding me that Watson was due for her rabies vaccination, as required by law in California, and a bright red envelope with a Queen Elizabeth II stamp bringing the first Christmas card of the season. I recognized the cramped handwriting as that of Great-Aunt Nell in darkest Sussex. I think she's under the illusion that the post still comes over on a steamer.

The business mail included a newsletter from Ferrets Anonymous reporting on the progress of attempts to legalize the possession of pet ferrets in California, and a postcard from a company in Illinois offering high quality and low prices on live-catch traps (from mouse to coyote), and specialty traps from snake to pigeon (no mention of those being live-catch).

Of particular interest were several lost-pet flyers from shelters and pet owners who would have picked up my name from my ad in a pet-resources directory. Though necessary to my work, it always saddened me to receive these. Buddy the Shar-pei gazed with haunted eyes from his flyer. Iniki the Siberian Husky, Gidget the red Pomeranian, in playful pictures taken in happier times. Would they ever get home? Time and again I noticed the line *no ID tag*. How could their owners ever expect to see them again, except by luck, random chance, the grace of God, or the observant deductions of Delilah Doolittle?

Cat flyers galore, I noted. Gracie, Bambi, Hector, Murphy, Sasha, Victor, Maynard, Austin. Cherished pets all. Such heartbreaking mail.

I looked at my watch. Heavens, it was nearly noon. The mail would have to be dealt with later. I quickly stuffed it back in the box, not wanting to lose any more time by returning to the house.

As Watson clambered into the back of the station wagon, I checked to see that I had the necessary equipment for catching an errant cat.

"We'd better take the 'come-along,' " I told her, picking up the catchpole (a long stick with a noose on the end of it) used to capture difficult animals.

"The heavy-duty carrier, too. If Meowzart is scared, he'll fight his way out of that flimsy cardboard thing in no time."

Watson looked a little disapproving, as if the less she had to do with such restraint-and-capture devices, the better.

As I drove I tried to recall what little I knew of Lizzie Walker. The day I met her she had been giving away kittens outside the local supermarket. A dumpy shape of a woman, her doughy face seemed to indicate a diet of doughnuts and cookies. Several of her front teeth were missing, the only colour on her pale face a smudge of misapplied lipstick or the residue of an orange breakfast drink, I couldn't quite tell which. Her grey, nearly white hair clung damply to her forehead in the summer heat.

Her clothes all looked as if they had belonged to somebody else, which they no doubt had, probably obtained from a thrift store. A stained (that breakfast drink again?) once-white blouse was rendered all the more ill-fitting by being buttoned one hole off target. Pale blue knit shorts clung less than seductively to chubby thighs and rear. The southern California climate encourages a minimal state of dress really suited only to the very young or the genetically blessed. Her age might have been anywhere between sixty and seventy-five.

She was holding a black cat with a white patch around one eye. It looked to be about six months old. Two younger kittens, black-and-grey-tiger-striped, peeped out from a cardboard box.

''His name's Spot,'' Lizzie had told me.

''Are you going to get the mama cat spayed?'' I asked.

''No,'' she said with a simpering smile. ''She's a Siamese. Usually the pet shop takes them, but they have too many.''

I wasn't surprised. Siamese or not, I thought, she's producing unwanted kittens. Giving them away like that, anything could happen. Would she ask questions of the new owners to ensure the well-being of these defenseless creatures? I very much doubted it. The unscrupulous could take the kittens and sell them to research labs. If children took them, there could be an unwelcome reception from parents. Thinking money might be the problem, I took out one of my cards and wrote down the name and telephone of a group that helped low-income people with spaying and neutering.

''Well,'' I said, doing my best to protect the innocent little faces that peered unknowingly from the box, ''do be sure not to give them to children without their parents' permission.''

''Children are kind to animals,'' she said.

''Please get the mother spayed,'' I returned, handing her my card. ''This place does it free.''

''She's a Siamese.''

It was as if we were talking two different languages.

What a pathetic figure, I remember thinking, my feelings a mixture of pity and irritation.

This was the woman I was about to ask if she had custody of Mavis Byrde's Abyssinian. Maybe it wasn't going to be quite so easy after all.

4

House of Horror

LIZZIE WALKER LIVED in Parkside, an older part of town where I had often admired the custom-designed homes, most built prior to 1940. At one time there had been talk of creating a preservation zone in the area, but now surveyor's stakes blossomed on several of the vacant lots and I recalled having read recently that the neighbourhood had been rezoned to make way for an automobile mart. A dismaying prospect.

Another disturbing thing was the proliferation of lost cat flyers—I counted at least ten—posted on the telephone poles and trees that lined the sidewalk. We were not far from Dog Beach and the feral cat colony, and I wondered if perhaps the coyote I'd seen that morning had passed this way in search of breakfast.

Lizzie's house must at one time have been quite charming. Situated on a corner lot, the three-storey structure still showed remnants of its former glory. A high turret window suggested what might once have been a sunny playroom; wooden shutters, many hanging half off their hinges, might once have framed windows through which an elegant home of style and grace could be glimpsed. A stand of cypresses, planted with pride so many years ago, left unpruned, now presented a formidable prospect to the street.

I parked in the shade of a massive jacaranda tree, its windblown blossoms, browned from the heat, strewn about the sidewalk. Rolling down the windows, I told Watson to stay put.

"This lady has a lot of cats," I told her.

Watson's ears perked up as she heard the word, but I knew she wouldn't budge unless I called her.

"We don't want to get off on the wrong foot. She's going to be difficult, and I don't think you'd be much help."

Watson knew the tone of my voice, and settled down with her chin resting on the window frame.

From Mavis's house next door the wind wafted the faltering tinkling of a piano lesson across her well-manicured lawn. I could see why she would be dismayed with her neighbour's neglect of her yard. She must have to fight a constant battle to keep the weeds at bay. "One-two-three, one-two-three. Lift those wrists," Mavis's voice came quite clearly.

I stepped cautiously down the litter-strewn path to Lizzie's front door, pushing past shrubbery that seemed to clutch at me from an overgrown planter. I pressed the doorbell, but no answering ring came from inside. The heavy knocker, stiff with age and dirt, barely responded to my efforts to knock loudly.

The door stood ajar. I pushed it open and called.

"Hello. Mrs. Walker. Anyone home?"

There was no response. I stepped into the hall. I was well aware that I was trespassing, but figured that my priority was to find Mavis's cat. If Lizzie appeared, I didn't think I'd have any difficulty talking my way out of trouble with the poor simple soul.

Though it was midday, the house was dark. As my eyes adjusted from the bright sunlight I made out newspapers piled head-high on either side of the hall. Numerous cats observed my entrance, some running along the top of the newspapers, following my progress, others content to sit and stare. I stared back, hoping to spot the missing Meowzart, but in the gloom it was difficult to make out anything but shapes.

The house fairly seethed with cats. They sat on the stairs, on and under the heavy Victorian hall stand at the end of the passageway. I had to avoid tripping over them as they ran under my feet. They reminded me of those puzzles in a children's book: how many cats can you find in this picture?

The farther I proceeded into the house, the stronger became the stench of feces and urine. I put my hand over my nose and mouth, removing it only long enough to swipe away the fleas that were now biting my ankles, or to call again, "Hello. Mrs. Walker?"

I peered into the first room I came to, which might have been a dining room at one time. The windows were covered in thick draperies, shredded at the bottoms by a thousand feline claws. A couple of half-grown kittens stopped their game of chase along the drapery valance and dropped at my feet. Others mewed quietly, as if in hunger. How could Lizzie afford to feed them all? Never mind the vet bills—if they ever saw a vet.

I made my way to the back of the house and the kitchen. I groped along the wall inside the door and flipped on a light switch. Cockroaches scurried away in every direction. Fighting down my own urge to scurry, I took in the scene. Fluff balls of cat hair rolled around the floor as I entered—which I did with extreme caution. It was almost impossible to avoid stepping into cat mess. In a cardboard box in one corner of the room, a mismarked blue-point Siamese nursed four tiny kittens.

I made my way back along the hall and up the stairs to the first landing, pushing open a couple of doors along the way, but the rooms appeared to be unlived in, except for yet more cats.

There were only two rooms on the third landing. The first door I tried was locked; the second opened onto a small room which I believed to be the turret room I had observed from outside, the window now draped in heavy black velvet. Up here a smell of incense mingled with the overwhelming cat stench. The room was lit by a single red, guttering candle, almost spent.

A woman who had apparently been kneeling in front of a simple shrine, appeared to have fallen forward, a prie-dieu overturned by her side.

I moved forward cautiously. "Mrs. Walker," I whispered.

No answer. I knelt down beside her. "Mrs. Walker? Lizzie? Wake up."

Gently I pushed on her shoulder to turn her over. Her eyes were wide open, as if in terror. Even before I fumbled for the pulse on her neck, I knew it was futile. Feeling something damp and sticky on my fingers, I recoiled in horror as I realized that blood had seeped from a wound on the back of her head.

As I wiped my fingers down the front of my blouse, the scene burned itself into my brain. At one end of the makeshift shrine, a heavy oak dining table, stood a brass candlestick, the initials *D.I.E.* engraved in its hexagon-shaped base. At the opposite end I could just make out an outline in the dust where its mate had stood. Illuminated by the flickering candle a tarnished silver frame held a photograph of a family group: a woman—Lizzie in her prime, perhaps—a tall fair-haired man, and two small children, a boy and a girl.

A sudden noise made me look over my shoulder in fear. It was probably only the cats, I told myself. But what if the murderer was still here? I had to get out of that house of horror as quickly as possible. With heart pounding, no longer concerned about where I was treading, I rushed down the two flights of stairs to the hall, stumbling over cats as I went. I had to find a telephone. The kitchen was the most likely place for one, but I didn't fancy any more cockroach confrontations, though creepy insects might be the least of my problems. I would call from Mavis's house.

I ran down the hall, flung open the front door, and practically fell into the arms of the man standing there.

5

Enter the Law

DETECTIVE JACK MALLORY was the first to recover.

"Mrs. Doolittle?" He raised shaggy grey eyebrows in surprise. "Where are you going in such a hurry? Are you all right?"

Did he think I was running away? No, of course not. How could he know about the body upstairs?

Surf City PD must have relaxed its dress code as a concession to the extremely hot weather. Mallory had shed his customary tailored sport jacket, and his short-sleeved shirt showed to advantage the muscular tanned arms now holding me in a bearlike grip on Lizzie's doorstep.

All this noted, I recalled later, as I struggled to regain my aplomb. It was some months since I had last seen Detective Mallory, and I had forgotten how circumstances always seemed to contrive for him to see me at my worst. Never more so than now, when I was shaken and disheveled from my headlong rush down the stairs.

"Lizzie Walker . . . dead . . . top floor!" I gasped.

With a sharp, "Wait here, don't go anywhere," Mallory pushed past me and took the stairs two at a time with an agility surprising for one of his age (mid-fifties, I guessed), and build (comfortable, to be kind).

Officer Bill Offley, who had come up behind him, eyed me suspiciously, echoed his boss's admonition to wait there, and lumbered up the stairs after him. He was panting by the time he reached the first landing.

Before long, first the coroner then the crime-scene crews and the various support personnel took over in a well-rehearsed performance of their duties, a process made all the more difficult by the high winds. Notebook pages were tossed, hats snatched, and doors slammed, in blatant disregard of the seriousness of the situation or the importance of the officials involved. Tempers, sorely tried by having to contend with the stench and the fleas, were close to the boiling point.

Mallory and Offley had been busy ever since they came back down the stairs, and Mallory, at least, must have trusted me to stay put, as I hung around ignored and, to all intents and purposes, forgotten while the investigation proceeded.

But I didn't deceive myself. I knew Mallory would get around to me sooner or later. And I was in no hurry to leave. I had a mystery of my own to solve. Where was Meowzart? I was hoping that all the disturbance might flush him out of hiding. So far, though, only one or two cats had escaped into the yard, none of them my particular quarry. Others, I guessed, would have retreated into various hideaways indoors as soon as the invaders stormed their peaceful domain.

I moved out of the line of traffic and waited in the shade of a cypress, near Mavis's, a vantage point from which I could keep an eye on both the house and Watson, still in the car. Though she watched the activity with interest, her eyes always returned to me, ever alert for a signal to call her to my side.

An old-established climbing rosebush, yellow, my favourite, grew against the corner of the house. The only plant surviving in the neglected yard, it had probably benefited from Mavis's lawn sprinklers. A stem, broken by the wind, hung limp, and I pulled it off, inhaling the flower's delicate perfume released by the hot afternoon sun.

From the moment the first police car had appeared, the sleepy neighbourhood had come to life. Ignoring police officers' requests to stay away from the scene, people seemed suddenly compelled to take their dogs for a stroll, to work in their front gardens, or to look for the postman.

Mavis waved at me from her front porch. Then she disappeared into the house only to reappear soon afterward and approach the low picket fence dividing the two properties. She was carrying an Abyssinian cat.

"Did you find Meowzart?" she asked, almost as if she believed the entire scene had been staged for her benefit.

"Isn't that him?" I asked.

"Oh, no, this is Depussy, Zart's twin. I brought him over so you'll recognize Meowzart when you find him."

She was wearing a low-cut, gauzy ecru top over a long

skirt, which blew fetchingly around her legs in the wind. A big, floppy beribboned sun hat framed her delicate face. There was a fragility, a vulnerability, about her that put one in mind of *Streetcar*'s Blanche DuBois. Though I had the feeling that this impression was probably as false as the long lashes that shaded her pale blue eyes, and that the lady, when push came to shove, would display the proverbial whim of iron.

"What's going on?" she asked.

I broke the shocking news that during my search for Meowzart I had discovered her neighbour's body.

"Oh, my goodness. How grotesque," she exclaimed, looking alarmed, as well she might, at the thought of a murderer on the loose in her neighbourhood.

I was about to ask her when she had last actually seen Lizzie Walker when I became aware that I no longer had her attention. She was looking at someone over my shoulder, and as her expression gradually changed from concerned to coquettish, I turned to see Detective Mallory approaching.

He nodded acknowledgment to Mavis, then: "Mrs. Doolittle, I must ask you to refrain from speaking to anyone until after I've taken your statement."

Mavis, obviously impressed by the detective's command of the situation, held out a delicate hand in greeting, which Mallory had not much option but to accept.

"Mavis Byrde," she said. "The concert pianist. You may have heard of me. I live here."

She held the cat against her face and looked up at him

through lowered eyelashes. The poor man didn't stand a chance.

I became conscious of my own utilitarian outfit. I must have looked like something a particularly undiscriminating cat from Lizzie's collection might have dragged out. Worse, I realized that they were both staring at the bloodstain on my shirt. I attempted to cover it by holding the rose against my body.

"I can't say I'm surprised." Mavis was talking about the murder. "It's been one thing after another over there. I've been dreading Halloween. I told her just a few days ago. 'Mrs. Walker,' I said, 'if you insist on lighting another bonfire on Halloween, I'm going to have to file a complaint with the fire department.' It's not safe, you know. Especially in this wind. It's so hard being a woman on one's own." She sighed with a wavering smile at Mallory, who smiled back sympathetically.

They both seemed to have forgotten my existence.

"And such odd behaviour!" Mavis continued, stroking Depussy who was getting restless. "She would just look right through you. And in all the time I've lived here she never smiled at me or said hello. She would just smirk."

"Did you notice anything especially unusual last night?" asked Mallory.

"Well, I think I should tell you that I did hear Lizzie arguing with someone," Mavis answered. "And that's not the first time. I've had to call the police several times to report yelling and carrying on."

"Can you describe the voice you heard on this occasion?" asked Mallory.

"It was a woman's voice. They were talking so loudly they woke me up, even above the noise of the wind."

"Did you recognize this other person's voice?"

"I might have, but I can't say for sure. I think it was that pet psychic woman, or fortune-teller, whatever she calls herself. Estelle LaBelle."

That was interesting. Could there possibly be a connection between LaBelle, with her claim to supernatural powers, and Lizzie Walker's reputation as a witch?

"What time was that?" asked Mallory.

"Quite late." Mavis patted her hair nervously with her free hand. "About midnight, I should say."

"Can you be sure it was midnight? Did you look at the clock?" I asked.

Mallory threw an irritated glance in my direction, and I realized I had overstepped the mark. Not wanting to give further offense, I held my tongue on the observation that when I discovered the body at about noon, the candle was still burning. If Estelle LaBelle or whoever the voice belonged to was the killer, and the murder had taken place around midnight, as Mavis's statement suggested, the candle would have been spent by the time I discovered the body.

Turning back to Mavis, the detective gave her a sweet smile that I didn't recall ever having seen before, and said, "Thank you, Ms. Byrde. I'll have an officer come by and get your statement later on. Meanwhile, if you wouldn't mind waiting at home?"

This last was uttered in the tone of a question, but there was no denying that it was a command. With a fluttery wave of her hand, Mavis tripped back through her English garden, along the crazy paving, through the rose-covered entryway, leaving a wafting of lavender perfume in her wake.

Mallory watched her go with a bemused look on his face, then turned back to me.

"Now, Mrs. Doolittle. Would you please explain how you happen to be here?"

"Actually, I was looking for a lost cat."

It was with what I considered remarkable restraint that he refrained from making an observation about that coincidence.

"Who let you in the house?"

"No one answered the door, so I walked in."

"In other words, you were trespassing."

"I was looking for a lost cat, and I had reason to believe that Lizzie Walker had possession of it."

Mallory said, "We'll get back to that. Now, where were you going in such a hurry when I arrived?"

"I was on my way to telephone you."

"There's a telephone in the kitchen."

"If you like cockroaches," I answered. Then, not without misgivings as to the tactfulness of my words, I said, "I could ask you the same thing. What brought you here?"

His blue-grey eyes indicated annoyance, but he answered amiably enough, "We were checking out an anonymous tip."

Though I would have liked very much to know just who the tipster was and what they had said, I realized that there was a limit to how much he might confide to me. Probably no more than he would to the newspaper reporters who would no doubt be showing up at any moment.

He brushed his thick grey hair, blown by the wind, out of his eyes, then asked, "Did you touch anything?"

Didn't he know me better than that? "Certainly not," I replied, bristling. "You're referring, of course, to the second candlestick? I hope you don't think I took it."

"You know it's missing, though?"

"Of course. I saw the dust marks at the opposite end of the table to where the remaining candlestick was, and assumed, as you have, that it was one of a pair."

"It's quite possible that it's the murder weapon," was all he said. He hesitated for a moment, as if considering his words, then said, "Mrs. Doolittle, I understand your concern in attempting to find somebody's pet, but I must warn you that any attempt to meddle in this case will not be welcomed, and could result in your being charged with interfering in police business." His voice softened a little as he continued, "There's a murderer on the loose, and I'd hate for you to be the next victim." He turned abruptly as Officer Offley came to fetch him back to the house.

After the paramedics finally wheeled poor Lizzie away, it was the turn of animal control to enter the arena. Mike Denver, shorthanded since the fire outbreak had required most of his officers to be sent off to rescue livestock, horses, and pets from the outlying areas, asked Detective Mallory to allow me to assist. No doubt recalling his last words to me, the detective took his time before nodding agreement. How much trouble could I get into with the police there?

I was only too pleased to help; it afforded me another opportunity to get into the house and search for Meowzart. Donning Hazmat-style gear of mask, booties, and gloves, I helped in the transfer of cats and kittens to the animal-control trucks lined up in the street.

We brought more than sixty cats out of the house that day, many suffering from mange, maggots, and malnutrition. Sadly, fifteen of them were so far gone they had to be euthanized immediately they arrived at the shelter, I learned later. The remainder were impounded, awaiting disposition by Lizzie's family, if such could be discovered.

The job was so onerous that at one point Officer Offley was called upon to help. But his handling of the catchpole was so inept that one cat got clean away, scarpering up the nearest cypress, where he stayed until the coast was clear, causing me to add under my breath a fifth *C* to my list of cautions for cats: "cops."

"What was that?" demanded a red-faced Offley.

"I said, would you like a hand?" I covered.

"Listen. When I need help from a pet dick, which won't be ever, I'll ask for it," he huffed, stamping his boots in a futile attempt to rid himself of fleas. Really, his insolence knew no bounds. I had no idea why he found me such a trial, and could only assume that his boss had shared his dislike of me on some occasion. Though I would have credited Mallory with more discretion.

AFTER WAITING SO patiently, Watson deserved a good run. I took her to Dog Beach, a section of Surf City's ten-mile strand that was set aside for dog walking. By the time we made our way past the cat colony and down the steep steps to the beach, the light was fading. There would only be time for a brief run before the sun dropped beneath the horizon. But it was too windy to stay long in any case. Windblown sand gritted my eyes. The only other person on the beach was a solitary surfer, his board buffeted like a sail as he made his way back to the parking lot. He must have been a novice; seasoned surfers would know the waves were too choppy. But the wind didn't seem to bother Watson, and we played until it was dusk and she could no longer see the driftwood I threw along the beach for her to fetch.

The sun had set by the time we climbed the steps back to the clifftop, and I had to step cautiously to avoid tripping. We had covered only a few feet along the path when Watson stopped in her tracks and uttered a deep low growl. I followed her gaze. In the gathering dusk, in the shadow of a clump of bushes, a coyote lurked. No doubt equally alarmed, he turned and took off at our approach.

6

Animal Talk

THE FOLLOWING MORNING most of the media led with the news of Lizzie Walker's murder. The *Los Angeles Times* carried a full report and a photograph of Detective Mallory over a quote that an arrest ''was imminent.'' I didn't believe it. Nothing I had observed at the scene led me to think that the police had the slightest clue of the murderer's identity. A neighbour was quoted as saying that there were rumours Lizzie had been the head of a witches' coven. ''Now she's gone, perhaps the cat killings will stop,'' the unidentified neighbour had said. How unkind, now that the poor woman was no longer able to defend herself.

I had been too tired the previous evening to do more than feed Watson, warm up a tin of soup for myself, and get to bed. But this morning, refreshed by a good night's sleep, I was ready to get back to work, beginning with returning telephone calls.

But first I checked the outgoing message, a weekly routine since the time when, after having received no calls for several days, I discovered that gremlins had chewed up the outgoing tape.

"This is Delilah Doolittle, tracer of missing pets. If you have lost a pet and have already checked your local shelter, please leave your name and telephone number, and I will return your call as soon as possible. If you have found a pet, please leave your name, number, and a description of the animal, then take it to the shelter, where its owner may be looking for it."

Everything seemed to be in order, and I played back the messages from the previous day.

Beep. "Delilah. It's Joan. Thanks so much for helping us out. Just wanted to let you know we're back."

The next two calls dealt with wildlife. A man from squirrel rescue informed me that he and his volunteers had trapped and released about one hundred squirrels during the last six days, saving them from the bulldozer that was grading over their habitat.

"Score one for the squirrels!" I said to Watson, who always seemed to enjoy listening to these communications about our kindred spirits. "Though I fail to see where we fit in." But really, was trapping and releasing wild squirrels any different from doing the same with feral cats?

Beep (a woman's voice): *"Is there anything you can recommend to keep the coyotes out of my yard? I love to see them, but one of them is eating the wild rabbits and stray chickens that live on my property."*

"Coyotes don't know any better, I'm afraid, luv," I said. "They're not vegetarians, you know." People love living close to our wonderful wilderness parks, but they want the picturesque kept at arm's length.

Beep (a man's friendly voice): *''Hello! I wonder if you might know where I could get a Siamese kitten for my mom. Hers had to be put to sleep recently, after sixteen years. Mismarked is okay, she says. But blue eyes are a must.''*

''Sixteen years!'' I remarked to Watson. ''That's a good home. We'll have to see what we can do.'' I thought for a moment. ''How about those kittens at Lizzie's yesterday? The mum was a Siamese. I'll take a look when I get to the shelter later.''

Watson wagged her tail as if in appreciation of a shelter rescue. A shelter alumna herself, she would know the importance of checking there first when looking to adopt a pet.

Beep. ''Dee, are you there?'' Evie's upper-class English accent pierced the air. *''Howard's got a few days off and we're taking the coast road to San Francisco. We'll stop by for a cup of tea and a tinkle the day after tomorrow.''*

Evie lived in San Diego, about a hundred miles south. Near enough that we saw each other reasonably often, but not so close that we were always on each other's doorstep.

''Oh, and be a sweetie and make an appointment with that pet psychic, Estelle what'shername,'' she continued. *''I'm worried about Chamois. He seems to have something on his mind.''*

Chamois was Evie's tiny Maltese terrier, who, as far

as one could tell, had very little mind to begin with.

Estelle LaBelle again. It was funny how her name kept cropping up lately. I hadn't thought about the pet psychic for months, and now her name seemed to be on everybody's lips. I was acquainted with her only through our common interest in finding lost pets—Estelle claiming to be able to communicate with animals through some kind of mental telepathy, while I employed the more conventional and physically tiring methods of interviewing, searching the shelters, distributing flyers, and studying the lost-and-found classifieds.

If Evie and Howard were arriving the following day, I'd better attempt a bit of housecleaning. The windows needed doing; I couldn't remember the last time I'd vacuumed; and my poor houseplants appeared to be undergoing some kind of near-death experience.

Not that the house required a great deal of attention. A pre-war bungalow I'd inherited from Roger, it consisted of two bedrooms, one of which served as an office and guest room for overnight visitors or the occasional orphaned pet, a comfy sitting room, and a kitchen just large enough to accommodate a small dinette set and an overstuffed, very worn armchair, which claw marks and dog hair identified as Watson's own. The best feature of the house was the back garden, an area, in stark contrast to indoors, that thrived on neglect. Overgrown with red bougainvillea and pink and yellow hibiscus, blooming year-round, it offered a cool haven in the summer, and in the winter a front-row seat of the migrating waterfowl which visited the neighbouring wetlands. The only things needing attention were the baskets of impatiens, fuchsia, and ivy geraniums that hung from the covered porch.

I decided to get up early the next morning and give the place a once-over before Howard and Evie arrived. And in case they decided to stay long enough for a meal, I'd stop by the British Grocer on my way home and get something that would do either for lunch or high tea: sausage rolls, maybe, or perhaps fish would make a nice change: kippers, maybe, or finnan haddie.

Today I had to do the rounds of the animal shelters to see if Meowzart or any of the other pets on my list had come in.

The weather continued hot and windy, and from my limited wardrobe I selected khaki shorts and a jungle-print blouse. My favourite desert boots would be the most comfortable and practical for walking around the shelters. Fortunately the job of pet detective required neither an extensive wardrobe nor, come to that, any particular qualifications other than persistence, a passing knowledge of animal behaviour, and a tendency toward eccentricity.

My faithful sidekick, Watson, trotted ahead of me out to the station wagon, and waited patiently by the rear door while I paused to enjoy the scent of the ocean carried on the gusty wind. I had been born and bred in the British Isles, a seafaring nation, and the ocean was in my blood.

Carried along with the salt spray came a disembodied voice from the lifeguard tower: "No dogs allowed on pier."

"You see, Watson," I said. "Now you've heard it for yourself. I keep telling you. No dogs allowed on the pier."

EVERY DOG RUN in the shelter was full. The combined emergencies of wind and fire had produced in the first place a lot of runaways, and in the second, rescues from homes in the canyon areas which were suffering the worst of the forest fires.

After checking the dog runs, I went to the cat room where in banks of cages a variety of cats waited to be claimed by their owners or, failing that, adopted. They ranged from the common domestic ("comdoms," in animal-control jargon) to the exotic, but there was no Abyssinian. Nor, I was surprised to note, the mama Siamese and kittens from Lizzie Walker's.

My next stop was the kennel office to check the DOAs and outside vet list. Though the shelter has a veterinarian on staff, pets picked up seriously injured are routinely taken to the closest animal hospital, rather than losing precious time transporting them to the shelter.

I always enjoyed talking to Rita, the obliging young woman with the ready smile who kept the kennel records. But it was a busy day at the shelter, and I had to wait in line while she attended to the customer ahead of me.

There seemed to be a problem.

"But I want the cat today," the woman was saying. "It's for my daughter's birthday. I suppose you'd rather kill it than put it up for adoption."

Rita took such barbs in stride. "I'm sorry," she explained patiently, pushing her heavy blonde hair back behind her ears. "It's our policy not to adopt out black cats during October. Because of Halloween, you know. We'll be happy to hold the cat for you until November."

It was unfortunate that it was necessary to protect black cats in this way. But there was no knowing what fate they might be released to at Halloween time.

It was strange how superstitions changed when one crossed the Atlantic. Here in America black cats were considered bad luck. But in England it was your lucky day if a black cat crossed your path. And at weddings the attendance of a black cat was considered as essential as that of a chimney sweep to guarantee a happy marriage.

There seeming to be no quick end to this particular dialogue, I sought out Mike Denver. I found him in the yard supervising the unloading of strays from the morning's shift.

A young animal control officer carried a trembling Sheltie mix in his arms. The dog's coat was severely singed. "Better let the vet take a look at him," said Mike. Then, turning back to me, he continued, "The fires have us run off our feet. Some folks are at work and don't know their homes are threatened, and their pets are left alone in the backyard."

The telephone rang. Something about horses trapped by fire in one of the canyons. Mike made some rapid decisions, stood, and went out to the briefing room to organize a rescue.

I made my way back to the kennel office to ask Rita about the Siamese cat and kittens from Lizzie's.

Rita's pink acrylic-nailed fingers tapped her computer keyboard.

"No record of them," she said. "It's possible that in all the confusion they were overlooked. There were so many. As soon as someone's available, I'll send them back to check. But with the fire emergency, I can't promise when. It may be a day or two. But they'll be okay. The guys left food and water in case we missed any."

I SPENT A restless night, dreaming about dead cats and howling coyotes. The noise finally woke me up and I realized that the howling was, in reality, fire truck sirens. A strange red glow was reflected on my bedroom walls. Pushing Watson aside, I got up and looked out of the window. The sky was ablaze. The wind must have shifted in the night, and the fire had licked down the canyons to the beach.

7

No Pets Allowed

I DRESSED QUICKLY and went out to the front yard, got the hose, and attempted to water down the roof. The water trickled out in a pathetic drip. Of course, the firefighters would be draining all available water supply to fight the fire, which, I saw to my alarm, seemed to be coming from the direction of the Surf City Trailer Park.

Returning to bed was out of the question. I would never be able to go back to sleep, and I felt I must stay alert in case some errant ember landed on my roof. Dawn found me outside surveying a yard, patio, and car covered with ash. The fire appeared to have been brought under control, though dark clouds of smoke still hung in the clear blue early-morning sky.

I was making a halfhearted attempt to sweep up the mess when I was surprised to see Howard's racing-green Jaguar pull up in front of my house.

"Thank heavens you're all right Dee," said Evie, getting out of the car and hurrying toward me. "As soon as I saw the fires on the news last night, I insisted to

Howard that we leave early this morning to check on you.''

Though she could still stand to lose a few pounds, my old school chum nevertheless looked very smart. Tanned and relaxed, the result of a recent holiday in Bermuda, she was dressed for touring in well-cut sage-green linen pants and a sleeveless top, the matching jacket to which hung on a padded hanger in the rear of the Jag. On her feet, close-toed shiny pewter sandals; around her neck, a string of cool sea-green beads that matched a ring on her well-manicured fingers.

The ubiquitous hat, this time a straw boater in a paler shade of green, topped her expertly dyed ash-blonde hair. Though why she needed to wear a hat in the car, I couldn't imagine. She soon enlightened me.

''I can't do a thing with my hair in this dreadful heat,'' she murmured as we kissed air. ''A trifle excessive for October, don't you think?'' Without waiting for an answer, she continued, ''Thank heavens for hats. Do you like this one?'' She tucked an imaginary stray wisp of hair back under the hat's brim. ''Neiman Marcus, on sale. Only a hundred and fifty dollars.''

''Cheap at half the price,'' I muttered. I wouldn't expect to pay one-fifty for an entire outfit. But everything was relative. Evie was a wonderful shopper, and she could sniff out a bargain like a terrier running a stoat to ground. Occasionally she would take me in hand and we would scout resale and consignment shops where she would outfit me with the most elegant, though inappropriate, outfits that it would never have occurred to me to put together. There's not much call for elegance in my line of work.

Howard, meanwhile, had come 'round from the driver's side of the car and greeted me with a warm hug. A tall rangy Texan and a man of few words—just as well, being married to Evie—he had proved a good friend to me over the years. A few years older than Evie, he was devoted to her, and she to him.

Reaching into the backseat of the Jaguar, Evie now brought forth a well-worn and decidedly unfashionable leather sport bag, which I knew to contain her treasure—Chamois, her Maltese terrier. He traveled everywhere in this bag. It was his second home. At their luxury condo in San Diego, he had the run of the house, but once they were away from home, as far as one could tell, Chamois's little paws never touched the ground. He went for more carries than walkies. Through the half-open zipper he looked up at me with button-black eyes, a permanent expression of surprise on his face, no doubt caused by the two red bows tautly pulling back his hair from a forehead permanently pink, the result of Evie's lipsticky kisses.

Watson, joining me in greeting our friends, nosed into the bag and gave Chamois a friendly nudge. The little dog responded with a yelp of terror.

When Evie finally paused for breath I said, "Yes, we're lucky we escaped. But I'm worried about Tony. The fire must be very close to his home." I pointed in the direction of the trailer park, less than a mile away, where a billowing cloud of black smoke made a sinister marker.

"If you wouldn't mind, I was just about to go over there to see if he's okay."

"Of course," said Evie. "I'll come with you. I'd love to see the dear boy again. Howard will stay here with Chamois, Watson too, if you'd like, and finish cleaning up for you." She turned to Howard. "Won't you, sweetie?"

Her husband had taken the broom from my hand some minutes earlier and was doing a good job of sweeping the front path.

Now leaning the broom against the garage door, he took the sport bag from Evie's hand, set it down, and encouraged Chamois to come out. The little dog obviously adored him, and came readily at his beckoning.

"He never does that for me." Evie pouted.

"That's because he knows you're going to lift him out," I said. "That dog's a lot smarter than he lets on."

"Well, I know something's bothering him. I hope you made that appointment with the pet psychic."

Actually, since I was not inclined to indulge Evie in such follies, I had let it slip my mind, but I didn't think there would be much difficulty getting in to see Estelle. After all, how many people were there, on a busy weekday, with fires to distract, who would be taking their pets for a consultation?

My ash-covered car not being fit for Evie to sit in, we took the Jaguar. Rather too elegant for me. We made an odd-looking couple—Evie with her slightly overweight blonde elegance, me five-foot-one if I stood up straight, in denim shorts, white shirt, and old tennis shoes.

"I think shorts after a certain age are most unbecoming," commented Evie as we drove off. She could always be relied upon for an honest opinion. I was reminded again of why, much as I loved her, I preferred her company in small doses.

"TIPTOE TONY" TIPTON, the dear boy of Evie's recollection, was neither a boy nor, as far as I was concerned, much of a dear. It was not entirely clear how he came by the nickname—whether from the way the senior surfer scampered, surfboard under his arm, across the hot sand like an aging sea elf, or on account of his reputation as a dip, or pickpocket, a career long since retired from, he claimed. A colleague of my late husband's, whose own business pursuits had occasionally been called into question, he was forever presuming on an acquaintance which should have ended when Roger died.

For some reason, though, Tony and Evie had hit it off from the start. It must be a case of opposites attracting, for apart from both being English, they had absolutely nothing in common.

Evie was born to the purple, as they say, a privileged only child of a titled family. We met at the private girls' school I was attending on a scholarship. I had been assigned to the house where she was head prefect, and she had immediately taken me under her wing, introducing me to that strange and somewhat overwhelming upper-class school culture that I, a child of working-class parents, suddenly found myself thrust into. The friendship had long outlasted our school days. We had both wanted to travel, and in our early twenties had come to the United States, where we had both married—she extremely well, myself not so, Roger having come to an untimely end after he fell in with what Evie refers to as the "wrong lot."

Nuisance though he was, Tony's cheery Cockney humour never failed to bring a smile, and I had to admit, he kept me in touch with my roots.

But it was a different Tony we encountered that day as we approached the fire-ravaged trailer park. Gone was the cheeky smile on his lined tanned face, the ready laugh, and the quick wit. In shorts and mismatched shoes, the few remaining gray hairs on his tanned pate appearing even more dissheveled than usual, he was leaning against a vintage woody station wagon which bore signs of serious fire damage.

He greeted me wanly, but his tired grey eyes took on a sparkle when he recognized Evie.

"'Allo, Mrs. Cavendish. Welcome to my 'appy 'ome," he said wryly, his Cockney accent causing the nearby firefighters who were checking gas mains to glance up in amusement.

"You poor thing," Evie sympathized. "It looks like you've lost everything."

"I saved me surfboard and me dog," he said. "That's all that matters."

The dog in question, Trixie, a white, black and tan

Jack Russell terrier, sat uncharacteristically quiet at her master's feet, as if she knew the import of the events that had unfolded during the night.

As I learned later, a sudden shift in the swirling Santa Ana winds had whipped the fire into a frenzy, quickly engulfing the trailer park. Before firefighters could bring the blaze under control, a number of mobile homes had been destroyed. Though Tony's trailer was still standing, it was going to take considerable repair. Plywood partitions had burned like tinder, and only the outer aluminum shell remained.

Fortunately there were no injuries among the hapless home owners, though some, including Tony, had fled their residences so quickly that they had no time to prepare or collect belongings. Still in their night attire, dazed looks on their faces, they sorted through rubble for a few remaining possessions.

A Red Cross field office had been set up, and volunteers were dispensing hot coffee and doughnuts, along with vouchers for clothing and information on emergency accommodations.

I could feel the hot ground burning through the soles of my shoes and moved to the wetted-down concrete slab that had been Tony's side yard. Evie followed me.

"Do you need a place to stay, Tony?" I asked.

"I'm going to bunk with me mate Sam for a few days. I'm waiting for him to come and pick me up now. Me car being out of commission, like."

I had heard Tony talk about his friend Slippery Sam Vyper in the past, though I had never met him. As far as I understood, he was quite a bit younger than Tony, more of an apprentice, one might say. However, any port in a storm, I supposed. I was relieved that he had somewhere to go; otherwise I would have felt compelled to offer him my spare bedroom.

But I wasn't about to get off scot-free.

"Only thing is . . ." Tony hesitated. "Only thing is, Sam's landlady don't allow no dogs, and I was wondering . . ."

"Of course, we'll be glad to take care of Trixie," put in Evie, bending down to pet the little terrier. "Won't we, Dee?"

I'm sure that given the opportunity, I would have offered, but I was irritated by Evie's speaking for me, and presuming that it would not be an inconvenience.

"If by 'we' you mean 'me,' of course I'll take care of her," I said, rather more tartly than I ought. It certainly wouldn't be the first time I'd cared for Trixie while Tony was indisposed. But his indisposition usually took the form of having been picked up by the police for some minor offense or another, he being one of the usual suspects rounded up whenever there was any trouble.

"Ta, luv," he said. "I don't 'ave none of 'er stuff, though. Her little basket got burned to a crisp. Thank Gawd she weren't in it at the time."

"Don't worry about that," said Evie. "We'll stop at the pet shop on the way back."

Actually there was no need to shop. I had plenty of supplies for a homeless pet—food, toys, bedding, leashes—but I didn't want to deprive Evie of a chance to do what she did best—shop. Little Trixie was in for a treat.

Other pets and their owners were not faring so well.

"I'm sorry," a Red Cross volunteer was saying. "Pets are not allowed in the evacuation center."

Residents holding dogs on leashes, or carrying cats in their arms, or birds in cages, stood around, uncertain of what to do in the face of yet another setback.

"That's outrageous." Evie's voice pierced through the confusion. "Pets not allowed, indeed. My friend here will be only too glad to—"

"No need for me to do anything," I broke in hastily, now recognizing her offer for me to take Trixie as the thin end of the wedge. "Dr. Willie and several of his colleagues have expressed willingness to house pets in an emergency."

I quickly wrote the vet's address on the backs of some of my cards and distributed them to the anxious pet owners.

" 'Ere comes Sam now." Tony nodded toward the park entrance, where a tall thin young man, still wearing what looked like the same grey sweats I had seen him in two days earlier at the feral cat colony, had just got out of a blue Toyota pickup. His feet were bare, and he hopped cautiously over the hot gravel. Attempting to keep his balance, he almost dropped the object he carried close to his chest.

8

Slippery Sam

HIDING MY SURPRISE, I smiled a greeting as Tony introduced us.

"This 'ere's me mate, Slippery," said Tony.

"A pleasure, I'm sure, Mr. Slippery," said Evie, for once in her life uncertain of the correct form of address.

Slippery Sam took the hand she held out in greeting, revealing, in the crook of his other arm, a ball python coiled like a huge knot.

The epitome of good breeding, Evie did not so much as blink. "How intriguing," she murmured.

It was then that I remembered why Slippery Sam Vyper, for such was his full name, had looked familiar the other morning. He was a reptile collector, and I had seen him once before at a herpetology swap meet when I was working on a case involving a stolen iguana. Why he felt compelled to carry the python everywhere he went, I could not imagine. I felt sure the poor creature would much prefer to be left alone in its tank than be handled constantly.

I reached out to touch the snake, running my fingers

tentatively along its cool, muscled coils, and thinking how my theory that over time owners and their pets developed a deepening resemblance to each other was reinforced by the lithe, almost sinuous movements of Sam's too-thin body. His pale face blended so well with his dishwater-blond crew cut that it was difficult to see where his forehead ended and his scalp began. One might guess he did not spend much time in the fresh air. His hooded lids over gold-flecked hazel eyes were half-closed, and when he finally spoke, his sibilant lisp, and his habit of running his tongue over his lips, enhanced the reptilian resemblance.

"No work today, then, mate?" asked Tony.

Sam shrugged, and muttered something about someone having called and canceled. It turned out he was an odd-job man, currently self-unemployed.

"Wasn't you s'posed to be working for Old Lizzie Walker this morning?" asked Tony.

Slippery looked at his friend from under hooded eyelids.

"She'th dead. Murdered."

Evie looked alarmed, but before she could speak, Tony said, "What! Why would anyone want to 'arm 'er? She didn't 'ave nothing worth stealing."

It crossed my mind that one might wonder how he was privy to such information.

"The police seem to think it might have something to do with witchcraft," I said.

"Witchcraft! That's barmy. 'S all the poor ol' dear

can do to get up in the morning and take care of them cats of 'ers.''

Sam nodded agreement.

Evie looked at me suspiciously. ''How is it that you're so well-informed?'' she asked.

Now I was in for it. ''It just so happens that I discovered the body,'' I admitted, trying to sound casual, yet realizing the impossibility of such a thing. ''I was looking for a lost cat at the time,'' I explained.

Tony and Sam regarded me with renewed interest.

''How did she die?'' asked Tony.

''She was struck from behind,'' I said. ''But I really don't think I ought to be talking about it.''

''Anything missing?'' Tony pressed for more details.

''A candlestick. The police think it might be the murder weapon.''

Sam shifted restlessly from one foot to the other, and I wondered if he knew more about the case than he was letting on, since he apparently had some connection with the murdered woman.

Evie was incensed. ''Really, Dee. Don't tell me you're mixed up in another murder case. I thought you'd have learned your lesson by now.''

My protests that I wasn't mixed up in anything, that I had merely discovered the body, reported it to the police, and that was the end of it, fell on deaf ears.

''I hope you have informed whoever it is that has been so careless as to lose their cat that you're giving up the case,'' said Evie. ''I insist on it. This pet detective business is much more hazardous than one might have expected. I really can't understand why Roger didn't leave you better provided for, but if you must work, then you'll have to find something more suitable. As soon as we get back, I'm going to ask Howard if he can get you something off the books.''

I really didn't care for her to be dressing me down in front of strangers, but fortunately Sam had wandered off to partake of the coffee and doughnuts being dispensed by the Red Cross volunteers. He certainly looked pathetic enough to qualify as a displaced person.

Evie looked to Tony for reinforcement.

''Tony, dear boy. I know you'll agree with me.''

Tony grinned. ''Don't you worry about our Delilah, Mrs. C. She's got a good 'ead on 'er shoulders, even if she do go off a bit 'alf-cocked at times.''

At least we'd got a smile out of Tony and distracted him from his misfortunes for a little while.

9
The Pet Psychic

WE HADN'T BEEN able to make an appointment with Estelle LaBelle until later in the day, too late for Evie and Howard to resume their journey north that evening. So with the convenience always at the disposal of the really well-off, they had opted to stay the night at their apartment at the Beverly Bayside Club in nearby Newport Beach, one of several residences they maintained throughout the world, including apartments in New York and London and a bungalow in the Bahamas.

After leaving Tony, we had, at Evie's insistence, taken a chance on a walk-in appointment to see if Amber could fit me in for a quick trim, shampoo, and set.

"You look ten years younger," Evie had said, surveying the result afterward. A dismaying thought. What on earth had I looked like before? My mind inexplicably returned to the recent scene in Mavis's front yard when Detective Mallory, obviously smitten with Mavis, would have ignored me altogether if I hadn't happened to be the one who discovered Lizzie Walker's body.

Howard, quite content to stay and watch a golf tournament on television, once again offered to pet-sit Watson and Trixie while Evie, Chamois, and I kept our late-afternoon appointment with the pet psychic.

Estelle had moved into the area a few years before, and though her name was well-known to me, for she had quite a following among the pet set, this was to be the first time I had visited her place of business. It was located in a two-storey white wooden building along Pacific Coast Highway on the outskirts of town, one of several converted beach homes, and sat between Sunny Sue's Middle Earth Florist on the one side and a realtor's office on the other. The freestanding sign on the pocket-sized lawn out front announced:

PALM READING
SPIRITUAL COUNSELING AND HEALING
FOR ANIMALS AND THEIR FAMILIES
BY APPOINTMENT ONLY

I had heard that Estelle was uncomfortable with the term *pet psychic,* being of the opinion that *animal communicator* would appeal to a broader segment of the pet-owning public. However she chose to describe herself, her gift for communicating with animals, though sworn to by some, was viewed with skepticism by others, myself included.

Evie was a true believer. I could have told her that the only thing wrong with Chamois was that he needed more exercise, more play, and if that didn't help, a trip to the vet. But she was convinced that something was bothering him, and Estelle would be able to tell her what that something was.

When I entered Estelle's parlour it took a moment or two for my eyes to adjust to the gloom after the brilliant afternoon sunshine. Black draperies hanging against all four walls shut out the daylight, and billowed in the draught as she closed the door behind us. A cut-glass chandelier with low-wattage bulbs hung above a maple-wood table, in the center of which stood the requisite crystal ball. The smell of scented candles was almost overpowering in the small, stuffy room, and I had the oddest feeling that I had been there before.

Displayed on a counter on one side of the room were items for sale, including crystals, jewelry, books on herbal remedies, and an assortment of scented candles, some lit, with names like Devil's Blood and Sorcerer's Elixir.

"So, you want to ask me about your dog?" Estelle said as Evie and I stepped carefully around the pentagram painted on the polished floor.

We had to strain to hear her voice. Low and husky, I took it to be part of the act. But maybe she had a cold. She did seem a little out of sorts. The wind was enough to get on anyone's nerves. I asked her if she felt all right.

She looked startled that I had noticed anything might be amiss. "Yes," she replied nervously. "It's just these Santa Ana winds. They set my teeth on edge. And the fires are getting dangerously close."

She was tall, above average for a woman, close to six foot I would say. And thin. She looked like a figure from an Egyptian frieze. Her thick black hair, streaked with grey, hung in a heavy long bob, a deep fringe valancing clear blue eyes. A silver necklace of stars and moons adorned her neck, and a dozen silver bangles slid along thin arms. I wondered why she felt the need to accentuate her height with the suede platform-soled shoes that peeked from beneath the hem of her long black cotton dress.

The little parlour was furnished with an eclectic assortment she might have picked up in a hurry at a thrift store. An ugly yellow vinyl couch stood against one wall. Two ill-matched chintz-covered easy chairs were placed on either side of the fireplace on which stood an embroidered fire screen bearing the words DO AS YE WILL, BUT DO NO HARM. I recalled having read somewhere that it was a tenet of modern-day witchcraft, and an unexpected shiver ran down my spine.

I took a seat on the couch. Evie chose one of the easy chairs then lifted Chamois from his sport bag and placed him on her lap. She rummaged through her purse; not finding what she wanted, she gave an exasperated, ''Blast. I've left my ciggies in the car.''

It was just as well. The room was stifling.

On the broad mantelpiece sat the largest cat I have ever seen—twenty-five pounds if it was an ounce, and black as Newgate's knocker. It stared at me with unblinking golden eyes, as if it shared its owner's ability to divine my innermost thoughts.

That was the disconcerting thing about psychics. Did they read your mind the minute you entered their orbit?

I hoped not. But the harder I tried not to think about the sallowness of Estelle's skin, and why she was wearing those ridiculous shoes, the more entrenched such thoughts became. I cast around for something impersonal to say. The cat reminded me of Mavis Byrde and the missing Meowzart.

Why not let Estelle know I was skeptical about her powers particularly as practiced over the telephone for fifty dollars per ten-minute session? That ought to shake her off track. Let her know I'd been called in.

"I met a client of yours yesterday," I said casually.

The blue eyes bored into my brain. "Mavis Byrde, of course," she said.

Evie shot me a look that said "I told you so," as Estelle produced this evidence of her powers.

I was shaken. "How did you know?"

"Obvious. The poor woman was frantic about her cat. It was only natural that she should explore every possible avenue. One doesn't need to be clairvoyant to figure that out," she said disarmingly.

Her bracelets jangled as she reached to pet the cat. "It would break my heart if I lost Wicca," she said.

"Wicca. What an enchanting name," said Evie.

"It means witchcraft," replied Estelle.

"How appropriate," I murmured. Everything seemed so calculated to fit the mood, right down to the cat's name.

"Now, Mrs. Cavendish, why don't you put Chamois on the table so I can get to know him," said Estelle, picking up the crystal ball and turning to place it on the display counter.

While Evie settled Chamois on the table I continued talking about my search for Mavis's cat, and how it had led me to discover the body of poor Lizzie Walker.

At the mention of Lizzie's name Estelle gave a gasp of surprise, dropping the crystal ball on the floor, where it shattered across the pentagram. Wicca fled, Chamois yelped in fright, and Evie and I looked at each other in amazement.

"What is it?" I asked, concerned. "Did you know Lizzie?"

Estelle just shook her head, hiding her confusion in the act of taking a dustpan and brush from the andiron set on the fireplace, and sweeping up the shards of glass. The chore gave her a chance to recover.

Evie was all solicitude. "My dear, do sit down, you look like you've seen a ghost," she said, unaware of the aptness of the simile. Then she turned to me. "It's all your fault, Dee. Talking about murders. Upsetting everyone. Poor Chamois is quite traumatized. We'll have to give him a few minutes to calm down. He's so frightened."

She put the little dog back in his bag, kissing and soothing him, then continued. "I know. Why don't we have our palms read while we're waiting? You first, Dee."

I'm not one to throw good money away on the dubious prospect of seeing into the future. If good is foretold, I'm set up for disappointment, and if it's bad news, then I'd really rather not know, thank you very much. But Evie was not one to brook an argument. She offered to pay, and before I knew what was happening, I was sitting at the table across from Estelle, with my palm extended.

"Now, Estelle," said Evie. "What do you see for Delilah? A really nice man, I hope. There has to be a suitable match for her somewhere."

Actually I wasn't sure there was any such thing as a suitable match for any woman if it's a man you're trying to match her up with. And I wasn't sure if any man was worth the effort. Though I remembered my marriage to Roger with fondness, perhaps its brevity had contributed to its charm. Who knows what irritating habits might have grated on the nerves of us both if he had lived? When I was young, my great-aunt Nell used to warn me that men only wanted "one thing," though what that one thing was she never made clear. But it seemed to me men, or more specifically, husbands, wanted a great many more things than one; dull things like meals on time, clean socks and ironed shirts, and their mother's birthday presents shopped for.

I was destined, however, not to have any RNM foretold that afternoon. The session was interrupted first by a knock, followed immediately by the opening of the door.

Once again Detective Mallory had caught me in an embarrassing situation.

10

Hocus Pocus

SUNLIGHT FLOODING IN through the open door showed Estelle's parlour for what it was. Ordinary, shabby, the black draperies nothing more than inexpertly dyed sheets.

Mallory in shirtsleeves, his loosened tie the only indication that the heat was getting to him, gave me the barest nod of recognition, perhaps as taken by surprise as I was by the encounter.

Estelle and I both stood up, she to greet the unexpected visitor, I to move back to my seat on the couch, in the forlorn hope that I might be regarded more as an onlooker than a participant in the interrupted palm reading.

Red-faced and sweating, the portly Officer Offley followed his superior into the room and plonked himself down on the vinyl couch at the opposite end to myself. As he sat, his weight forced the air out of the cushions, and I felt myself sliding toward him. Close contact with Officer Offley not being something I craved, I clung tightly to the couch arm. That and my sweating bare legs saved me from slipping farther, but I nonetheless felt gauche and uncomfortable, and found myself wishing I'd followed Evie's advice and worn slacks.

Mallory addressed Estelle. "Ms. LaBelle?" She nodded. "Detective Mallory, Surf City PD." He showed her his badge. "I'm investigating the murder of Mrs. Elizabeth Walker of Walnut Avenue. We have a witness who claims that you were at the deceased's house on the night of October nineteen."

"Excuse me, Constable," protested Evie. "But you seem to be unaware that you are interrupting a private meeting."

Mallory regarded Evie with the same quizzical expression with which he had favoured me on more than one occasion.

"What do you know about the case?" he asked her.

"Not a thing, thank the Lord," replied Evie. "But we have waited all day for this appointment, and I don't appreciate—" She sounded the *c* in *appreciate* like an *s,* rendering her voice all the more supercilious.

"Well, I'm sorry about that," Mallory interrupted her. "But we don't investigate murders by appointment."

From his seat on the couch, Offley wiped his sweating brow with the back of his hand and added, "We're here on official business, not hocus pocus." From the sport bag came an uncharacteristic growl, and Offley looked around for the source of this challenge to his authority.

Five people, a dog, and a cat were a few too many bodies in that tiny overscented room. It was claustrophobic, and we were all very hot and uncomfortable.

Evie, once again groping in her purse, pulled out a tiny gold cigarette lighter, looked at Mallory, and asked, "You wouldn't happen to have a cigarette, would you?"

Mallory, startled, looked at me as if for an explanation of my friend's behaviour.

Seizing the opportunity to get out of my seat, I stood up and said, "Detective Mallory, you may remember meeting my friend Evie Cavendish previously."

The detective gave no indication that he remembered her, though I didn't believe for a minute that he did not. With Evie it was a case of once seen never forgotten, and Mallory was far too astute not to have filed her away in his memory bank.

Evie held out her hand. "Mrs. Howard Cavendish," she said, "of the Houston Cavendishes." They shook hands, then after putting her finger to her chin, Evie pointed it at the detective. "Mallory? Irish. Are you by chance related to Sir Hugh Mallory of County Cork?"

Evie could be a first-class snob when the mood struck her, which it obviously did at that moment. But this time her snobbery backfired.

"Second cousins," replied Mallory, giving as good as he got. I wasn't sure if either one of them was telling the truth, to be quite honest, as somebody has to be.

Mallory swiftly returned to the point of his visit.

"Sorry about the interruption, but this is police business. There's been a murder, and palm readings and the rest"—he cast a look in my direction—"will have to wait."

Offley, meanwhile, had left his seat on the couch,

which creaked and groaned as if with relief, and was investigating the room, looking behind the draperies, inspecting the fire screen, making his own notes.

Mallory addressed me. "Might I ask what you are doing here, Mrs. Doolittle?"

Oh dear. It suddenly occurred to me that he might well think that I had come to warn Estelle, having been privy to Mavis's statement that she had heard her quarreling with Lizzie the night she was killed.

"I should think that's perfectly obvious," chimed in Evie before I had a chance to answer. "We are in the middle of a séance."

We were not in the middle of any such thing, and I really was getting cross with her. Mallory must think I was the most bubbleheaded person he'd ever met. It seemed to be my fate that whenever our paths crossed, my friends were in some way or another doing their utmost to make me look ridiculous.

But Mallory gave no further indication that he had any interest in my activities whatsoever, Evie's explanation apparently having sufficed. He turned to Estelle.

"Ms. LaBelle. We have a witness who says she heard you arguing with the deceased that evening."

"Did your witness see me?"

"No. She heard raised voices, and thought that she recognized one of them as yours."

"Then your witness is mistaken," said Estelle calmly.

Mallory looked at his notes. "Would you mind telling us where you were during that evening?"

"I went to South Coast Plaza to do some shopping. I

had a meal, then went to the movies.'' Her voice was so low, we all had to strain to hear.

''Did you go with someone?''

''No. I was alone.''

''What movie?''

Evie stood up with a snort of impatience. ''I say, this is the height of impertinence,'' she burst out.

Offley looked up from the display counter, where he was sniffing at the Devil's Blood candle, and said, ''Sit down and be quiet, ma'am.''

Evie appeared to be on the verge of a tart retort, but a stern look from me caused her to think better of it. She sat down again, with only a muttered, ''Don't ma'am me,'' followed by something about a ''corpulent copper,'' which fortunately only I was able to hear.

Estelle also attempted to calm Evie. She waved her thin hands gently, indicating that she had no objection to the questioning. ''It was the revival of *Indochine,* at the art house in the village,'' she said.

I wouldn't have figured Estelle LaBelle for a foreign-film aficionado, nor very likely to spend several hours wandering around a shopping mall, but one should never make snap judgments about people—something, along with jumping to conclusions, I was all too prone to do. I had no reason to doubt her. But Mavis had seemed so sure. However, I also recalled how spiteful she had sounded when making her accusation.

ESTELLE REMAINED REMARKABLY calm after Mallory and Offley left, almost as if their visit was something she had anticipated and prepared for. She insisted that we continue with the palm-reading session. But I was equally insistent that we put the whole thing off until another day. Take a rain check, as they say in America. A phrase I'd never had occasion to use until that moment. It so seldom rains in southern California.

It was quite evident Evie had taken a dislike to Mallory, and voiced her opinion on the way home.

"I think you're rather too taken with that policeman," she said as she steered the Jaguar down Pacific Coast Highway. "Blushing like a schoolgirl every time he spoke to you, or even looked in your direction. I won't have you falling for him, Dee. Just consider what you're about, my girl. It won't do, you know. It won't do at all."

She paused as she negotiated a lane change in readiness for the right-hand turn into my street, then continued. "I shan't visit you any more if this is how you're going to carry on. Every time I come here there seems to be murder and mayhem afoot, and policemen around every corner. It's just not on."

But I was scarcely listening. I was still hung up on her suggestion that I was interested in Detective Mallory.

"Such a thing has never entered my mind," I protested vehemently. Or if it had, it seemed that I was so often at a disadvantage when our paths crossed that the possibility of the attraction being mutual was patently absurd.

11

Coyotes or Cultists?

It was a day or two before I saw Detective Mallory again, and when I did, it was, once more, quite unexpected.

Howard and Evie had resumed their journey to San Francisco, taking in Carmel and Monterey along the way. Evie rang from Carmel to report the weather divine, no fires on the horizon, and not a policeman in sight.

I had to admit I missed her bright chat and candid observations, but as I said to Watson and Trixie, who had paused in their standoff over Watson's chair when the telephone rang, we had work to do.

Matt and Matilda, the two Malamutes, were still at large. Then there was the Boxer that had been reported missing after its owner returned from a week's business trip. She had left the feeding of the dog to an eleven-year-old neighbour who had failed to lock the back gate one night after feeding. Since the boy was too scared to tell his parents that the dog was gone, it had been three days before the alarm was sounded.

And, of course, there was Meowzart. True to feline form, he seemed to have vanished without a trace. I only hoped he hadn't ended up as coyote food.

Mavis had telephoned a couple of times to check on my progress. On the second call I could tell she was harbouring similar fears.

"Are you coming to the meeting tonight about the missing cats and cat killings?" her little-girl voice whispered over the telephone.

I had been so distracted by Lizzie Walker's murder, and by the arrival of Evie and Howard, that I had forgotten all about the meeting. "That's tonight?"

"Yes. With Halloween coming, some of the neighbours think the cats have been taken for use in ritual sacrifice. We're demanding that the authorities do something about it. Animal control is sending someone to talk to us. I'm so afraid Meowzart has fallen into evil hands."

I was sure that the cat killings had more to do with coyotes than with cultists. Ceremonial killing of animals may be all very well in some parts of the world, but where I come from it is simply not done, and neither did I believe it was being done in Surf City.

But I did think that it behoved me to put in an appearance at the meeting. It was good to keep informed, and I might pick up on something about Meowzart. It could also be good for business, I thought as I tucked a few extra business cards into my purse.

While I sympathized with Mavis about her missing pet, I was really quite put out with her. I felt she had spoken out of turn, accusing poor Estelle of being involved in a horrible crime. I was sure the investigation should be going in a different direction. Where, for instance, was the second candlestick? Of course, if it was the murder weapon, the killer would have disposed of it by now. Dropped it off the end of the pier, more than likely. That's what I'd do, I thought, a little shocked that I even entertained such a notion.

THE MEETING WAS held in the community room at the Parkside branch library. Someone had brought cookies and punch, and paper plates and napkins, bright with Halloween themes, dotted the room.

Joan and Bill Anderson waved to me from the far side of the room. To judge by their casual clothes, I guessed they had come straight from their evening feeding of the ferals.

Detective Mallory was near the door, leaning against the wall, eyeing with distaste the contents of the plastic cup in his hand. It was probably wishful thinking on my part, but I thought he brightened up when he saw me.

Mavis fluttered toward us on impossibly high-heeled sandals. She was wearing a low-cut, frilled-yoke brown satin blouse over tight leopard-print pants, her grey-blonde hair caught up in a brown velvet scrunchy. Not my style at all, though some, including perhaps Detective Mallory, whose arm she took in a surprisingly familiar manner, might find her mode of dress rather alluring.

''What a wonderful turnout. I love a crowd, don't

you? It takes me back to when I was on the concert stage. I'm a classical pianist, you know," she said, glancing up at him through those false eyelashes of hers.

Looking a trifle hunted, Mallory gently extracted his arm. "So you mentioned before," he said.

Surely he could see through her wiles? But then, men rarely do, do they?

"To think it might be a wild animal killing our poor kitties," Mavis trilled. "It's shocking. So distressing. Do you know, one time I saw a coyote blithely jump over our six-foot back fence."

"How do you know he was blithe?" I couldn't help asking. "The poor thing was probably scared out of its wits."

Mavis looked a little taken aback, and gazed around as if to see if there was anyone else in the room worth attaching herself to.

"It takes all sorts to make a world," said Mallory, smiling, his eyes following Mavis's slender figure as she tottered back into the crowd to greet a friend.

True. But one wondered whether quite so many sorts were necessary.

Soon after, Mallory excused himself and joined a group of animal control officers on the far side of the room.

It was an informal meeting, and apart from the officials, who took their seats on the platform, most people stayed by their chairs when they stood to speak.

The evidence for witchcraft was flimsy and appeared to be more the result of neighbours harbouring grudges against Lizzie Walker and her alleged coven than anything tangible. Everything pointed to the coyotes. A young police-sergeant liaison with the local Neighbourhood Watch team, stated flatly that no practitioners of witchcraft were known to be residing in the area.

One woman, who said she had found the remains of a cat in her yard, asked why, if it was the work of a coyote, it wouldn't have eaten the entire carcass?

"Not necessarily," replied Dr. Willie, our veterinarian and local wildlife expert. "Maybe something disturbed it while it was eating. Or, if the animal was careless, he might drop the carcass on his way back to his den, especially if he was frightened by people or dogs." Dr. Willie had discarded his customary wet suit for well-fitting jeans and a navy-blue long-sleeved shirt, which, open at the neck, set off his olive complexion admirably.

Mavis, who had moved over to my side again, eyed the vet appreciatively. "What a hunk," she murmured. "Alas, just a teensy bit too young for me."

Bill Anderson stood up. "If it's coyotes, what can we do?" he asked; concern for the ferals was clearly on his mind.

"There are no simple solutions," said Mike Denver, speaking for animal control. "We're getting more calls about coyote sightings every day, especially since the fires have broken out. So don't leave food out, secure garbage-can lids, and keep your pets indoors." He emphasized this last point by thumping the fist of one hand against the palm of the other. "Outdoor cats have a real short life span, for a lot of different reasons. Neighbours may trap and dispose of them. They may get hit by a car or be taken to the animal shelter. But the coyotes get the blame."

"How about trapping?" someone else asked.

Dr. Willie fielded that one. "Trapping seldom works," he said. "That just leaves more food for the survivors. They're healthier, and have larger litters as a result. And if we didn't have the coyotes, we'd have a real rodent problem. You can't remove one strand of the web without the rest of it collapsing."

One man, complaining that he had lost one cat to a coyote, suspected that to have been the fate of another, and now was concerned about a third.

"Some people are slow learners," I murmured to Mike Denver, who had moved across to my side of the room, balancing a cup of putrid-looking orange punch, a napkin, and about six chocolate-chip cookies in his big hands.

The meeting broke up soon afterward, people having to be satisfied with Mike's promise to assign an extra patrol to the Parkside neighbourhood.

"How's the investigation going?" I asked Mallory, who had appeared at my side as we made our way to the door. "Did you find the missing candlestick?"

"All I can say is that we've made an arrest," he said.

I gave an involuntary gasp. "Not Estelle," I said, recalling his recent visit to the pet psychic.

"That's all I can tell you." He looked around for a trash bin, disposed of his punch cup, then nodded good night and pushed ahead to the exit.

At first I was inclined to take his abruptness personally, but then I turned and saw what I guessed to be the real reason for his hasty departure. Mavis had him in her sights once again.

12
Ladybug Days

THE WEATHER CONTINUED hot and windy, almost daily sparking new fires in the canyons and forests. Fallen leaves, dry as potato crisps, rattled along the sidewalk, and Trixie would break into a fresh outburst of barking at every gust of wind.

Watson and Trixie were not the most compatible of roomies, the Dobie aloof and mature, the terrier high-strung and constantly on the lookout for mischief. But I made allowances for her, knowing how she missed Tony. Every so often she would stop what she was doing (usually tormenting Watson), stand stock-still for a moment, listening, then jump up onto the sitting-room sofa so that she could look out of the window. As she was doing the afternoon following the community meeting.

"What is it, Trixie?"

I was soon enlightened. A few seconds later Tony's woody, now running but still in need of a paint job, pulled into the driveway. Shortly thereafter, Tony himself appeared at the kitchen door. He had obviously just come from the beach. He was wearing his short-legged summer wet suit, his few remaining strands of curly grey hair pressed damp against his head, his rubber thongs tracking sand into the kitchen. That was one of the drawbacks of living at the beach. Sand got into everything. It grated underfoot, was ground into the carpet, clung to beach towels, and thence made its way into the washing machine and dryer.

"Where's me dog, then?" said Tony as Trixie bounced excitedly at his feet.

"Here, girl," he said, tapping his knees, bending them slightly. Trixie flew into his arms, nearly knocking the spindly Tony backward in her exuberance.

"She heard you coming," I said.

" 'Allo love. How's tricks?" I wasn't sure whether he meant how was Trixie, or the more conventional salutation.

"You've been surfing?" I said. It was more a reproach than a question. "I'd have thought you'd be too busy getting your place back into shape."

He had the grace to look shamefaced. "Primo conditions. Can't 'elp meself, luv. It's ladybug days, you know."

Sometimes, in a strong offshore wind, the pretty little red-and-black insects (ladybirds, we call them in Britain) are helplessly borne toward the ocean and can be seen clinging to every available surface along the shoreline—on surfboards, signs, lifeguard towers. Surfing conditions are often at their best at this time, and "it's ladybugs" becomes the code for perfect, three-foot offshore peaks.

Trixie was showering Tony with doggie kisses. "Nah,

luv. Leave off now. Did you miss yer old man, then? You'd think I'd been gone a month, instead of a few days,'' he said, obviously as pleased to see his dog as his dog was to see him.

He looked at me hopefully. ''Any chance of a cuppa?''

I had already anticipated the question and was plugging in the electric teakettle as he spoke.

''How're the repairs on your place coming?'' I asked, reaching into the cupboard for an extra cup and saucer. The question was not entirely altruistic. The sooner he was able to move back into his trailer, the sooner I would be rid of my canine houseguest. Trixie was a little love, but she missed Tony, and relieved the boredom by pestering Watson. She was younger than the Dobie by several years, and had energy to spare. All Watson wanted was peace and quiet. She didn't get much of either with Trixie around.

''Can't do much till I get me insurance claim settled,'' he answered.

I opened a packet of Walker's shortbread and we sat at the kitchen table, Tony dipping the rich buttery biscuits into his tea.

But he looked troubled. He seemed subdued, and his grey eyes had none of their usual merriment.

''What is it, Tony?'' I finally asked. ''Is the insurance company giving you a hard time over your claim?''

''You 'aven't 'eard, then? It's me mate Sam. The police have picked him up in connection with old Lizzie Walker's murder.''

''Go on,'' I said.

'' 'Sright. Seems he 'ad this 'ere candlestick which he pawned down at the local Uncle's. Apparently the police was looking for it.''

''So that's who Mallory was talking about,'' I murmured, half to myself.

''What?''

''Nothing. Carry on. You were saying . . . the candlestick?''

''Easy enough to trace, acourse, since Sam didn't 'ave no idea. And when they came to the 'ouse, he didn't bovver to deny it was 'is.''

He poured some tea into his saucer and set it on the floor for Trixie. She lapped eagerly.

''Do you think there's a chance he killed Lizzie?'' I asked.

''Not on yer life. Ol' Sam wouldn't 'arm a fly. All he cares about is that there snake of 'is.''

''How did he explain the candlestick, then?''

''Says Lizzie gave it to 'im for doing some yard work over there.''

Recalling the overgrown state of Lizzie's yard, I found it difficult to believe that she even cared about having any work done, much less hiring, as in paying, someone to do it.

''He swears that palm reader woman, Estelle what'sername, hired him,'' Tony said. ''That's how come he was working for Lizzie.''

This was getting odder by the minute.

"Thing of it is," Tony went on, "I was wondering if you could 'elp us out, like?"

"But what can I do?"

Tony explained that with Sam in the clink, the landlady wanted no more to do with him, and planned to rent out his room. "So she's giving me the elbow."

Tony paused expectantly, and it dawned on me that he was hoping he could stay with me. An alarming thought. Hedging, I said, "When do you have to get out by?"

"She's given me to the end of the month. The rent's paid up till then. Acourse, I have to take care of the bleeding snake as well." He grimaced. "Don't know as I 'ave the stomach to feed it a rat, fresh or frozen." He smiled wryly.

"I'm expecting Howard and Evie back at the end of the week, and they're planning to stay here for a few days," I lied. Trixie was one thing. Tony, his sand, and his surfboard quite another. I had my limits. Obviously the best way out of the dilemma was to solve the mystery of Sam and the candlestick.

"The last I heard, Detective Mallory was zeroing in on Estelle LaBelle," I said, and went on to tell Tony about Mallory's visit to the palm reader's the other day.

"Well, if that don't take the cake," said Tony. "What was he after?"

"Mavis Byrde, Lizzie's neighbour, swears she heard Estelle and Lizzie arguing on the night of the murder, so they wanted to question her about her whereabouts that night."

"And . . . ?" Tony prompted.

"Estelle says she was at the pictures. But she had no witness."

"Did you believe 'er?"

"Not really. She was too glib, as if she'd memorized the whole thing. And now you're telling me there's a connection between her, Sam, and the candlestick. But if Sam's telling the truth, the date on the pawn ticket will prove it." I leaned forward and patted Tony's arm. "Don't worry. The police will figure that one out soon enough. What I'd like to know is why anyone would want to kill Lizzie in the first place."

"Strange old bird, that Lizzie," he said. "Always traipsing around with a pramful of cats."

"Well, I suppose she thought she was doing the right thing. She took them in."

"They took 'er in, more likely," scoffed Tony. "Place to live, three squares a day. Very cushy." He picked up Trixie's saucer, then went on. "Have they done the autopsy yet?"

"Blow by a blunt instrument, I believe."

"That's why the cops are so interested in the candlestick, then." He grinned. "Thought it might 'ave bin fur balls wot got 'er."

As soon as Tony left, I headed for Estelle's place. My curiosity was getting the better of me. Why would Estelle hire Sam to work in Lizzie's yard? What business was it of hers anyway? If Sam was telling the truth, there must be a connection between Estelle and Lizzie.

I took a chance and left Watson and Trixie at home. Settling them each with a dog biscuit—Watson in her chair, Trixie in the guest bedroom in the comfy sheepskin designer bed that Evie had bought for her. They were both sulking, Trixie because Tony had left without her, Watson because she didn't get to go with me so often when the little terrier stayed with us. "You have to baby-sit," I told her.

I arrived at Estelle's a little after dusk. The wind had done considerable damage since my last visit. The palm reading sign had blown over, and a trash can rolled aimlessly back and forth across a lawn littered with rubbish. No light gleamed through the black drapes or the chinks in the doorway.

Altogether the place had an abandoned look about it, an impression that was reinforced by the scrawled note, apparently written in haste, tacked to the front door: *Closed until further notice.*

13

The Lady Vanishes

WHERE WAS ESTELLE? I hoped she hadn't taken off as a result of Detective Mallory's inquiries. Nothing could be more indicative of guilt. Or, one supposed, of innocence.

If, as the note suggested, she was to be gone for an extended period of time, she might well have informed her neighbours, perhaps asking them to pick up her mail or her newspapers. Or, at the very least, to keep a friendly eye on the place.

I crossed the paved driveway separating the two cottages to inquire of Sunny Sue at Middle Earth Florists.

A brass bell tied to the door with a rope of macramé announced my arrival. The overwhelming smell of a potpourri of rose, gardenia, and jasmine hung in the air-conditioned plant-filled room. Do cut flowers really retain their scent for a prolonged period, I wondered, or was this a marketing ploy, the florist enhancing the effect by periodically spraying the premises with a few squirts from an aerosol can?

A woman emerged from a back room. She was wearing a green linen apron with capacious pockets from which hung pieces of raffia and ribbon of various colours. A pair of scissors hung on a ribbon around her neck. If this was Sue, she looked more surly than sunny that day. I guessed business was slow: in that heat who wanted flowers destined to wilt before one reached home?

"May I help you?" she said eagerly.

"I hope so. I'm looking for Estelle LaBelle from next door. We had an appointment," I fibbed, "and she seems to have forgotten all about it."

"She's gone," Sue replied, obviously disappointed I was not a customer.

"Do you happen to know where she went? It's most important that I get in touch with her."

"No idea. She keeps to herself. Hope she's gone for good. That place gives me the creeps. Bad for business, having a witch next door."

"She's a palm reader, not a witch," I said. "Surely there's a great deal of difference."

"I don't care what she calls herself. She's a witch. Have you seen inside that place?"

"Yes, I have. Harmless window dressing, I'd call it. We all have to do what we can to bolster the image," I said, pointedly sniffing the fragrance-laden air.

Still, I was sorry to disappoint her, and looked around for something to buy to make up for it, settling on a small mauve African violet. Not a wise choice. African violets are notoriously hard to care for, and it was doomed to certain death in my hands.

As I paid Sue for the plant I gave her my business card, saying, "If you should happen to hear from Estelle, I'd appreciate it if you'd give me a call."

ARRIVING HOME I read the note *care instructions for your new plant* and put the violet on the sitting-room shelf I had long ago designated "plant death row." Why did I buy it? I asked myself as I surveyed the other plants in various stages of neglect. It was a weakness of mine. I was forever buying plants for which I had neither the inclination nor the know-how to care for properly.

Was I once again to be guilty of planticide? Conscience-stricken, I took a pitcher of water from the kitchen and refreshed them all, then turned to my desk to play back my messages.

Beep. "Hello. Delilah. This is Hannah from the San Lorenzo Humane Society. We have your flyer about the Malamutes. There's a couple here that could be the ones you're looking for. We'll hold them till we hear from you."

San Lorenzo was a small coastal town in San Diego County, about fifty miles south of Surf City. It was too late to go there that evening. I'd leave first thing in the morning.

I had just put the phone down when Mavis called. "Delilah. Any news of Meowzart?"

"I'm doing everything I can. I've checked the shelters and placed ads in newspapers from here to San Diego and Los Angeles. And you must have seen my flyers posted all over town. They're bright green. I'm sorry to disappoint you, but I did warn you, cats are really difficult to find. Are you sure you've searched your house thoroughly? Maybe he managed to get himself locked in a closet."

Mavis assured me that she had checked every nook and cranny in the house. "But you're right," she said. "Cats can get into some extraordinary places." She paused. "Come to think of it, Estelle did say he was in a dark place."

A thought occurred to me.

"Speaking of Estelle," I said, "I've been trying to get in touch with her, but it appears she's left town. Do you happen to know where she might have gone?"

"I couldn't say," Mavis replied. "Though I do remember she once said she had friends—or relatives, can't remember which—in San Diego County somewhere. Winona, I think it was." She sighed audibly. "Never mind about that woman. What about Meowzart? I have him entered in the national cat show coming up at the convention center. He's certain to do well. You must find him in time."

I hated to tell her I had serious doubts that I was going to find him at all. Never mind in time for the show.

14

False Starts

"BLAST," I SAID, as the turn of the ignition key yielded nothing but a depressing hiccup.

There are three things that can get my day off to a bad start. The first occurs when there's no milk for my morning tea, on this occasion having run out as a result of my unexpected teatime visit from Tony the previous afternoon; the second occurs when the car won't start. The third occurs when both of these things happen on the same day.

Having settled for tea without milk, I was all set to drive to San Lorenzo to check out the Malamutes, Watson waiting expectantly in the front seat of the wagon, Trixie bouncing around in the back. I had left a note on the door in case Tony came by, telling him that he would find his dog at Dr. Willie's. I had no alternative but to board her for the day. There was no knowing the disposition of the two Malamutes I hoped to be bringing back with me, and I had no confidence at all that Trixie would be good. Misbehaving dogs in cars make for hazardous driving.

A couple more fruitless tries at starting the engine convinced me I was wasting my time. The petrol gauge registered three-quarters full. Perhaps it was the battery, or something electrical? There was no way of knowing. Much as I admire today's young women who are as familiar as their boyfriends with what goes on under the bonnet, I had no wish to emulate them. One cannot be expected to be an expert in life's every arena. Having been raised in a country where transportation necessitated no more knowledge than the location of the nearest bus stop, I make no apologies for my ignorance. Me and technology just don't get along. That's why God created the automobile club.

While I waited for the tow truck, I checked the Pacific Telephone yellow pages for car rental agencies. Not an expense I wanted to incur, but I needed to get those Malamutes back ASAP. Clyde's Renta Clunka ("Don't let the name fool you") sounded the most in tune with my budget.

Joe Briggs, the local Triple-A representative, greeted me like an old friend. As well he might. I had probably paid the down payment on that new house he and his wife recently moved into. He knew my car's inner secrets much better than I. After unsuccessfully attempting to jump-start the battery and peering under the bonnet for several minutes, he finally shook his head, backed up his truck, and prepared to tow the wagon to his repair shop.

• • •

CLYDE INGRAM, THE proprietor of Renta Clunka, delivered the rental himself. Figuring I could pass some of the expense along to my client, I had decided to splurge on a minivan. I already had Watson and my equipment to take. Returning with two large, possibly unruly Malamutes would require something spacious.

At first glance he looked familiar. Since he was a local businessman, it was quite possible I'd seen him around town, perhaps pictured in the local newspaper or at some community event. Tall and angular, mid-forties, with light brown hair, thinning and starting to grey, he wore a sour expression, as if out of sorts with the world. Not particularly conducive to good business, I thought.

There was a certain arrogance about him, too, and I took immediate objection to the way, with misplaced gallantry, he addressed me as "little lady." It's true I am of less than average height and, I trust, a lady, but that's entirely beside the point.

He did, however, help me to transfer my pet detective gear from the driveway where Bill had piled it for me.

He sneezed as he lifted the cat carrier. "You had a cat in here?" he asked.

"That's what it's for. Are you allergic to cats?"

He sneezed again. "Sure ab," he said. Taking a small plastic spray bottle from his pocket, he held it to his nose and squirted a couple of sprays into each nostril. "Been doing it a lot lately. Must be the weather."

I agreed that the winds that had been plaguing us all week long would be laden with plant allergens. Just this morning the television weatherwag had referred to higher-than-average pollen levels.

Clyde sneezed all the way back to the rental lot and I was afraid it was the cat carrier rather than the high pollen count that was to blame for his current discomfort.

"Do you often suffer like this?" I asked.

"Ever since I was a kid," he said, taking his hand off the wheel to rub at red, watery eyes. "Got to get to the doc for another injection."

In his office I signed the necessary documents allowing me to take the van on the road, and I told him I expected to keep it no more than a couple of days.

"No probleb," he said, and sneezed again as he saw me to the door.

I DROPPED OFF Trixie at Dr. Willie's, then stopped at the bank for some ready cash. I had my credit cards, but I would have charges to pay for the Malamutes. Boarding and impounds, possibly rabies injections if they were no longer wearing their license tags as proof they'd already been vaccinated, and any veterinary care they may have needed after their adventure could run into two hundred dollars or more. Most shelters did not take credit cards, and might well refuse an out-of-town cheque.

I had forgotten all about Halloween, and when I entered the bank, it was somewhat disconcerting to find the custodians of my money wearing fancy-dress costumes. Accustomed as I was to the staid staff of Barclay's, the London, Midland & Scottish, and Westminster banks, the informality of American banking personnel is something I've never been entirely comfortable with.

A witch with long green talons reached for my withdrawal slip. In a greasy black wig topped by a pointy hat, she was quite unrecognizable as Mary, the fresh-faced young woman who usually helped me. I wouldn't have known her except for the pumpkin-shaped nameplate on the shelf above her station. I looked to the bank manager for reassurance, but she had metamorphosed into Morticia Addams. In a black formfitting dress with a plunging neckline, she sat behind a spiderwebbed enclosure, casting her spell over a computer keyboard. I was thankful I wasn't opening an account that day. Handing over two forms of ID, my Social Security number and my mother's maiden name to a witch would have been a little unnerving.

Eventually, all business taken care of, I set off for San Lorenzo. The amiable Watson lay beside me, her head resting in my lap. The long drive gave me the leisure to try to make sense of all that had happened since I had discovered Lizzie's body.

I spoke aloud to my canine sidekick. "It's far from elementary, my dear Watson." She had been dozing but raised opened eyes toward me at the sound of my voice.

"Suspects, you ask? Well, there's the anonymous tipster, for one. Who was that, and how else could they know about the murder, unless they did the deed? But then, why would they tip off the police? Perhaps it was a third party who arrived before I did, discovered the body, and not wanting to be involved, tiptoed out again. Could it have been Mavis, looking for her cat? Then setting me up to find the body?''

Watson did her best to look interested, though I could tell it was all a bit beyond her.

''And do we believe Mavis, who claims to have heard Estelle arguing with Lizzie? What possible motive could the pet psychic have, and what's all this about Sam and the candlestick?

''Maybe Mavis did it. Perhaps the dispute over the cat got out of control, and now she's trying to throw suspicion onto Estelle.'' The more I thought about it, the more it seemed possible that Mavis might be the murderer. Though she didn't look strong, she was very determined, and more than a match for the frail, aging Lizzie. And, maybe, she had an accomplice.

''Well, it's no use us worrying our heads about it, Watson, old girl. It's police business, as Detective Mallory is only too fond of pointing out to us. And we have our own cases to solve. We have Matt and Matilda to find.''

15

Road Rage

THE SAN LORENZO shelter was small compared with the Surf City facility, which, in a tri-city agreement, also served two neighbouring towns. There were only two aisles of kennels, lined with dog runs on either side, and it didn't take me long to spot the Malamutes that Hannah, the shelter manager, had reported. Almost immediately I was sure they were Matt and Matilda. They were still wearing the broad red leather collars the owner had described, but no tags, only empty S-hooks hanging from the metal rings. I prefer split rings to attach tags to collars. Much more secure. Even so, it would be a real coincidence if both had fallen off in the past few days, and I suspected that the dogs might have been stolen sometime during their adventure and the tags removed. Then, perhaps proving too much for their abductor to handle, they had been dumped in the street, far from home.

Hannah unlocked the kennel gate for me, and I leaned over to pet first Matt, then the slightly smaller Matilda, riffling through their coarse, wolf-grey fur to verify the identifying marks the owner had told me about. I leashed them both securely, paid their "bail," and returned to a patiently waiting Watson, settling them in the back of the minivan behind a portable metal pet barrier. Acquired specifically for the station wagon, it wasn't a perfect fit, but I managed to wedge it in such a manner that, provided the Malamutes didn't conspire to launch an all-out attack, it would hold.

It was early afternoon. I had enjoyed the smooth ride down the coast in the air-conditioned minivan and was in no hurry to return it. Matt and Matilda, probably relieved to be out of the shelter and sensing they had found a new friend, quickly settled down. Watson, as always, was content to be by my side.

Reluctantly I headed for the freeway, but before I reached the on-ramp for Interstate 5 north, I saw a sign for Escondido and, on an impulse, headed inland instead.

"It's too tempting," I said to Watson. Escondido, a few miles inland, was the location of my favourite English bakery. It was lunchtime. Sausage rolls would go down well about now.

A short time later I parked the minivan in the shade opposite the bakery and hurried across the street to make my purchases. Steak-and-kidney pie, sausage rolls, and Eccles cakes.

I stopped at a Jack-in-the-Box drive-through to pick up hamburgers for the dogs, and we had a picnic in a public park near the town center. After giving one another a few exploratory sniffs, the dogs got along quite nicely, and we took a leisurely stroll around the shady park. Then it really was time to be getting back.

"Okay, lad and lasses, we'd better get going before the rush hour starts," I told them.

Getting out of town was trickier than I had expected. I had forgotten the route since the last time I was there. The Malamutes, restless after their walk, refused to settle down again and proved to be a distraction. I took a wrong turn, went east when I should have gone west, and found myself driving through rural northern San Diego County.

I wasn't worried. It was good to be out in the country, and I was enjoying my drive past farms and ranches. Hedges of red and orange bougainvillea and pink and white oleander lined the highway that climbed gently to hills covered with terraced avocado and orange orchards, with mountain vistas on the horizon. It was hard to believe that Los Angeles was not much more than a hundred miles distant.

"We'll come to a freeway direction sign sooner or later," I told my canine companions.

After several attempts to find my way back to Escondido had failed, however, I began to regret my decision to take a jaunt.

"Maybe at the end of this lane . . ." I murmured to Watson, who shifted restlessly.

But at the end of the lane I came to a T-junction and had no idea whether to turn left or right.

Not only that, but I began to get the distinct impression that I was being followed.

I had been about to pull over and consult a map when

I became conscious that a truck that I'd been watching in my rearview mirror for the last few miles was now so close it was in danger of running into me. I turned right, hoping the driver would be going in the opposite direction, but he followed right behind.

In my rearview mirror I could see a large black truck. A rack of deer antlers adorned the top of the cab, and something that looked suspiciously like a rifle hung behind the driver's seat.

He honked as if wanting to pass. I slowed down, intending to pull over, but he just came up closer behind me. I stepped on the petrol pedal, trying to pull ahead, but he started gaining on me again.

Suddenly the truck hit my rear bumper with a force that made me bite my tongue. Matt and Matilda tumbled forward, loosening the partition, and poor Watson fell to the floor. Without waiting for the dogs to regain their collective balance, I pulled ahead again, driving as fast as I could, hoping to keep away from this madman until I could find some assistance, preferably in the form of a passing police car.

What was his problem? Was he drunk? Or was this road rage, the latest phenomenon to hit the southern California highway? People becoming so impatient with events they were unable to control in their lives that they were ready to take offense at every real or imagined highway discourtesy, and to take out their frustrations on total strangers.

I reviewed my drive through Escondido. I had been going slow, looking for the right turnoff, but I didn't recall having done anything to offend. I admit to not being the fastest driver on the road; neither did I care to be. But I considered myself a good driver, and had just recently completed the 55 Alive course at the Surf City senior center.

I dismissed the suspicion that this was a personal attack. No one knew I was driving a rented car. If anyone did have it in for me, they'd be looking for my Ford Country Squire wagon, not a minivan.

The narrow two-lane road began to corkscrew upward into the mountains. The minivan did not take kindly to the steep incline, and on unfamiliar roads, I was terrified of oncoming traffic, or that a deer or rabbit might choose that fateful moment to cross the road.

Sensing trouble, the three dogs were now all on their feet, slipping alarmingly from side to side of the van as we rounded the narrow mountain curves. The flowering shrubs I'd admired just a short time earlier now rushed past in a blur of pinks, reds, and greens. Quaintness turned to menace as guard rails came dangerously close.

I became convinced the madman was trying to force me off the road, and that I would tumble down a mountainside, later to be found dead, the dogs turned loose to become victims of mountain lions.

It all came to a screeching halt when, rounding yet another breathtaking bend, I saw a barricade across the road and a fire marshal's sign with the words FIRES. DANGER. NO VEHICLES BEYOND THIS POINT.

16

A Chance Encounter

I PULLED UP sharply, inches from the barricade. Matt and Matilda fell against the partition, dislodging it permanently this time. I put out a hand to stop Watson from falling on the floor again, but was unsuccessful.

In the rearview mirror I saw my pursuer pull into a lay-by, do a quick U-turn, and speed away in a cloud of dust and gravel. My question why, now that he had me trapped he didn't close in for the kill, was soon answered. I looked up from helping Watson to see a man in the uniform of a San Diego County sheriff's deputy. He tapped at my window. I lowered it and he peered into the car, backing away immediately at the sight of the three dogs—Watson recovered, ready to leap to my defense if I gave the word, the Malamutes growling.

"Where d'you think you are? The Indy 500?" he said. Though his tone was jocular, his face showed concern.

"There's a man following me. Trying to run me off the road," I said, my voice trembling.

"I didn't see no one," he replied, wiping sweat off

his brow with the back of his hand. "Too busy jumping out of your way."

My request for an escort back to the nearest police station was met with little enthusiasm. They were on full fire alert, the deputy explained, and unable to spare anyone. He did, however, call in a report to the California Highway Patrol, and with that I had to be satisfied.

Amid admonitions to drive carefully, I did a U-turn and ventured cautiously back in the direction I had come, keeping a sharp lookout for the madman.

A few miles farther along the road, after first assuring myself that he was nowhere in sight, I pulled into a picnic area to take stock. Miraculously none of us was hurt, though there was a lump forming on my forehead where it had hit the windshield when I pulled up sharp at the fire barricade. And my stomach felt queasy; I was regretting scoffing down those sausage rolls.

I let the dogs out for some exercise, then rearranged the stuff in back of the van, returning the metal partition to its original position.

Matt and Matilda eyed me gravely as I secured their leashes to a car door handle while I worked. Who was this woman who was taking them on such a wild ride? they must be wondering, perhaps starting to think longingly of the safety of the animal shelter they had left an hour or two earlier.

When all was shipshape again, I sat down on the grass to rest. Watson lay by my side, and I stroked her head as I digested the events of the last hour. It was peaceful just to sit here and listen to the birds singing, and the ripple of a brook rushing over boulders and pebbles a few yards away, and I was reluctant to get on the road again.

Finally, when my pulse had returned to normal, we got ready to leave. A sign at the exit from the picnic area indicated Highway 76. I knew that would lead me to the freeway.

After driving a few miles, I came to a junction with a sign that read WINONA, POPULATION 976. Winona. Wasn't that where Mavis had thought Estelle LaBelle might have gone? With a population of so few people, she shouldn't be too hard to find.

I could hardly ignore this unexpected opportunity to have a quiet word with her, to find out whether Slippery Sam was telling the truth when he claimed that she had commissioned him to clean up Lizzie's yard. If I needed further justification for my "meddling," as I was afraid Detective Mallory would regard it, the detour would allow me to put more distance between myself and the pursuer in the black truck.

There was not a soul about on the dusty main street of the sleepy little town, lying quiet in the autumn heat. My first stop was at a telephone booth to consult the directory. I wasn't surprised to find that there was no listing for LaBelle. I never had believed that to be her real name.

Petrol was getting low and I stopped at the first, quite possibly the only, service station in town.

I was relieved to see that the single pump was of the old-fashioned variety, not one of those newfangled machines where you put a credit card in a slot and hope for the best. One of the things I had enjoyed most on first arriving in California was the service. Austerity still reigned when I left England, and driving into a California petrol station for full service—windows washed, the tires and everything under the bonnet checked—was a revelation. But after the gas crisis of the seventies, things changed. Automation took over, stations switched to self-service, and I had to learn to pump my own petrol.

A young woman came forward, the name Lisa embroidered on her overall pocket. "Hello. Fill 'er up?"

"Thank you. Where is everybody?"

"Staying close to home. Fires. My dad's a fire spotter over on Lookout Mountain. Says if the wind shifts we'll be right in the path."

After dispensing the petrol and washing the windows, she took my credit card and said, "What brings you to Winona?"

"I'm looking for a friend who's visiting family in this area. Her name's Estelle LaBelle."

Lisa shook her head. "Don't know anyone with a fancy name like that. Only people 'round here with a visitor today is the Nolans. I think Nancy's mom is visiting. You might try there. They have a place down the road a piece. Last house on the left on the way out of town. Can't miss it. Sign out front says rabbits and goats for sale."

Lisa was right. The Nolan place was easy to find. I parked across the street in the shade of a large oak tree, cracking the windows for the Malamutes.

Taking Watson with me, I crossed the street. There were several cars parked in the driveway: a small workmanlike pickup truck, an older-model red Honda Civic, and a peacock-blue Ford Escort sedan, one of which might well belong to the mother-in-law. I had never noticed what kind of car Estelle drove.

A sandbox and brightly painted swing set in the side yard indicated young children in the family.

Out front a man who appeared to be in his early thirties looked up from where he was tending a rabbit hutch, feeding the occupants some kind of hay or alfalfa. He watched my approach across the street with apparent interest.

He brushed his hands against each other and closed the hutch door as I made my way up the gravel driveway. Maybe he thought I was a rabbit customer.

His pleasant "Can I help you?" turned to "Whoa" as he got a good look at Watson, alert by my side.

"She's quite harmless," I assured him. "Here, Watson, shake hands."

With perfect manners, Watson sat, then extended a paw, which the man good-naturedly accepted.

"Pleased to meet you, Watson," he said with a grin. Then to me: "Are you interested in the rabbits?"

"What kind are they?" I asked, peering into the hutch at the black-and-white bunnies pulling on the alfalfa.

"These are dwarf Dutch. But if you're interested, I've got some minilops in the back."

"Do you sell them for pets, or for meat?" I asked.

"Only for pets. The women in the family"—he nodded toward the house—"my wife, daughter, and mother-in-law, wouldn't let 'em go for anything else."

I liked this young man already. I decided to be honest. "Lisa at the gas station suggested you might be able to help me. She said you have a visitor. I'm looking for an Estelle LaBelle."

He looked puzzled. "No one's visiting here, except my mother-in-law. Her name's Mary Walker."

Even then I didn't twig immediately. Walker was a common name. In fact, I was about to go back to the car when the front door opened and a woman called out, "Lemonade, anyone?"

The deep, husky voice was unmistakable.

"Mom," the young man said. "This lady's looking for someone named Estelle LaBelle. We don't know anyone with a fancy name like that, do we?"

Gone were the trappings of the palm reader and pet psychic. No long black dress, no jangling silver jewelry. In their place baggy jeans and a bunny T-shirt. Her hair was caught in a ponytail, the long fringe pinned back on either side of the blue eyes with a child's barrettes. A very ordinary-looking woman, a little taller than most, to be sure, but definitely momlike.

Realizing that I had been on the verge of betraying a secret, I tried to cover my tracks. I had already found out quite a bit more than I had expected to when I left home that morning, and would be satisfied with that. What business was it of mine if Estelle had a secret life? Detective Mallory would find out soon enough, if it was important to him. I didn't want to be the cause of family strife.

"I must be mistaken, then," I said to the young man. "Sorry to have bothered you."

I returned to the minivan and was readying myself for the drive home when I looked up to see Estelle standing beside the car.

I lowered the window. "Estelle, I'm sorry. I didn't realize I was barging into a family situation."

She spoke to me in lowered tones. "There's a Tastee-Freez about a mile east of here. I'll meet you there in half an hour."

Before I could say yes, no, or maybe, she was back across the street, walking past her son-in-law's puzzled gaze without looking at him.

17
A Revelation

So it was that across a dusty picnic table beneath a willow tree at the Winona Tastee-Freez, with Watson, Matt, and Matilda lying at our feet, I learned about Estelle's double life.

''You understand that what I'm about to tell you is in strict confidence,'' said Estelle, her thin, high-cheekboned face lined with anxiety.

I nodded slightly, not wishing to voice agreement to anything until I knew what it was.

''This is where I was the night of the murder.'' She seemed relieved that she could finally confide in someone.

''You lied to the police, then. But why?''

''I couldn't let my family know about my other life in Surf City.''

''What, that you're a pet psychic, a fortune-teller? What's so shameful about that?''

''You don't understand,'' she murmured.

''I will when you explain,'' I said, a trifle impatiently. Then, in an attempt to get her started, I went on: ''Mavis

Byrde seems positive that it was you she heard arguing with Lizzie the night of the murder."

"She's heard us in the past, but not that night."

"Why would Mavis lie about something like that?"

Estelle sighed. "You'd have to ask her that," she said. "I honestly don't know why. Perhaps she really was mistaken. She has complained to the police about it before."

As Mavis had so pointedly stated to Detective Mallory. Something he would have confirmed by now, I was sure.

"What would you be arguing about with Lizzie Walker?"

"It was about the cats again, trying to get her to reduce the numbers, get them altered. Clean up the place."

"But why were you so concerned?"

"She was my mother."

Well, you could have knocked me down with a fevver, as Tony would say. It was true, one never could tell about people.

Estelle proceeded to sketch in the details of her secret life. She had lied to protect her family, telling her daughter, the child of a youthful indiscretion, that her father was dead and, not wishing to burden her with a crazed grandmother, that there were no other living relatives.

Estelle's mother had divorced and remarried when Estelle, Mary then, was about five years old. Her mother's new husband, Dennis, also had a child, a boy of about her age, of whom he had gained custody when his ex-wife committed suicide shortly after their divorce.

The second marriage had been a mistake from the start. Lizzie was obsessed with cats even then, causing her stepson much misery because of his allergies. The young Estelle had planned to leave home as soon as she finished high school, a plan that was accelerated when a teenage romance ended in pregnancy.

"A foolish teenage encounter," she said, using her hands expressively, though she seemed to recall the boy had been more committed to the relationship than she. She had never told him or her mother about the little girl she had borne at a home for unwed mothers in San Lorenzo.

It had been hard, raising the child on her own, but she had managed somehow, getting a job waiting tables, attending night school, first taking a secretarial course and later exploring her interests in animal health and psychology. Once her daughter was grown and happily married, Estelle had returned to Surf City to keep an eye on her aging mother, and to see if she could make a living with the animal communication skills she had developed over the years. She had changed her name because she didn't want her relationship with her mother to become known, choosing Estelle LaBelle as suitably exotic for someone dealing in the psychic mystique.

"I guess I inherited my love of animals from my mother, though I hope it never turns into the kind of obsession she had." She smiled.

I shook the ice in the bottom of my lemonade cup.

"More lemonade?" I asked her, standing up, ready to go for refills.

By way of assent, she gave me her empty cup.

When I returned, Matt had left his place in the shade of the picnic table and was resting his head in Estelle's lap, his soft brown eyes speaking affection.

"He's so glad you found him," she said. "They've had a very scary time." She reached out to pet Watson and Matilda, who had come forward for their share of attention.

I had not said a word to Estelle about the identity of the dogs or where they had been.

"He told you that?" I asked, eyebrows raised. I hoped Watson wasn't about to share any of our secrets.

Estelle nodded. "After the garage door blew open, they ran along the bike path beside the flood-control channel until they came to a road with a lot of noisy cars." She paused in petting the three dogs and looked up at me. "That's probably Pacific Coast Highway. Some people in a truck stopped and put them in the back. They took away their ID tags. The people were arguing and talking about selling them to a research lab. Matt and Matilda were really frightened, so when the truck stopped at a traffic signal, they jumped out. Then the dog catcher got hold of them."

It was a plausible tale. I might have guessed at a similar scenario. But I'd had previous knowledge. Estelle knew nothing about them being in a garage, or the San Lorenzo shelter, or even that they were not my dogs.

I had to admit I was impressed. "How do you do

that?'' I asked. ''How can they communicate with you?''

''With pictures, not words,'' she said. ''It's like watching a television screen. They hope you're going to take them back to their real home.''

''I've been telling them that all afternoon,'' I said. ''We've just had to take rather a long way 'round.''

Estelle took a sip of her lemonade, then continued her story.

''I learned later that my stepfather died a year or so after I left home. It was a freak accident. He tripped over one of the cats on the upstairs landing, fell down the stairs, and broke his neck.''

It was Estelle's opinion that guilt had been a contributing factor in her mother's eccentric behaviour which had worsened over the years. Even changing her name back to that of her first husband, Walker, in an attempt to wipe out the memory of the second, hadn't helped.

''Lately she'd been delving into witchcraft, hoping to communicate with my stepfather, wanting him to forgive her. It seemed harmless enough. Just a simple altar, the candles, a photograph of mother, Dennis and me and my stepbrother.''

I hesitated before my next question, trying to find words which wouldn't offend.

''You don't think there was any truth to the accusations of ritual sacrifices, do you?''

Estelle recoiled in horror. ''Oh, no. Nothing like that. My mother loved animals.''

On her return to Surf City, Estelle had been dismayed

to find her mother living in such squalor. Though she did not care to advertise the relationship, she visited her frequently, usually at night. The visits inevitably ended in arguments about the conditions her mother chose to live in.

"I was trying to get the place cleaned up. I hired someone to do the yard work."

I put down my empty lemonade cup and looked at my watch. It was growing late, and I needed to get Matt and Matilda home, but I wasn't finished.

"That brings me to why I'm here in the first place," I said. "I feel I owe you an explanation, having stumbled onto your secret and almost blown your cover."

I gave her an abbreviated version of how and why I had sought her out. How I had gone to San Lorenzo to pick up Matt and Matilda, got lost leaving town, saw the sign for Winona, and took a chance I might find her.

"But why did you need to see me?"

"I'm helping a friend, Sam Vyper. He claims that you hired him to clean up your mother's yard, and that she gave him a candlestick in payment."

She looked surprised. "I'd already paid him. Gave him twenty-five dollars. I don't know anything about giving him the candlestick. But that's the sort of thing my mother might have done."

"Well, Sam's in a lot of trouble over that candlestick, and I really think you ought to tell the police about it. And you must tell them where you really were on the night of the murder."

"Oh, no, I can't do that. I could never let the family know the truth."

"Look, they're going to find out anyway, if you get arrested for murder. The police are trying to verify Sam's alibi. How long do you think it's going to take them to locate you?"

She was reluctant, but it was clear to me that she could see the sense in what I was saying. "I'll do it. Just give me a day or two to prepare the family," she said. With that I had to be satisfied, and changed the subject slightly.

"Do you have any idea who might have killed your mother, or what possible motive the murderer could have?"

She shook her head. "Mother could be very difficult at times, and her behaviour was erratic. There were endless complaints about the condition of the house and the yard. But I know of nothing that would make anyone want to kill her."

It struck me that Estelle's talent for reading minds must be limited to animals. Otherwise, surely, she would have picked up on something that would give out such strong vibes as a murder must, especially a murder of someone close to her. Unless she wasn't telling me the whole truth.

But something else had apparently occurred to Estelle. She thought for a moment, then continued, almost as if talking to herself. "I do believe she feared something like this might happen, though."

"What makes you say that?"

''Last Halloween she'd celebrated with a Samhain, or 'summer's end,' bonfire. It's an ancient custom where you throw a marked white stone into the flames. If the stone can't be found in the ashes the next day, it's supposed to be an omen that the thrower will die before the following Halloween. When I visited her a day or two later, she was terribly upset, hysterical almost. She hadn't been able to find her stone.''

An unfortunate superstition, I agreed.

Estelle continued her story. ''Mother calmed down eventually, but she was never able to put it out of her mind entirely, and had been marking off the days until this coming Halloween, when the curse was supposedly to be lifted.''

I gathered up the dog leashes and prepared to leave.

''By the way,'' I said as we made our way to our cars. ''What is the significance of the engraving on the candlestick—DIE?''

Estelle eased her long legs behind the Escort's steering wheel.

''That's the monogram from my mother's second marriage—Dennis and Elizabeth . . .''

The last word was lost in the noise of the motor as she drove off, and I wasn't sure I'd heard correctly. But what I thought she said gave me much to ponder on the way home.

MY PROGRESS BACK down the mountain was slowed briefly when I encountered two California Highway Patrol cars. A black truck, with deer antlers on the cab, was wrapped around a tree, and the officers appeared to be in the process of apprehending the driver. The madman had got his comeuppance, apparently. A fact confirmed by a report in the next day's *Times* that he had been arrested after police had received several complaints of a man in a black truck pursuing and assaulting lone women drivers in northern San Diego County.

18

Happy Returns

MATT AND MATILDA were on their feet whimpering with excitement as we approached their home. I had trouble clipping the leashes to their collars, they were so eager to get out of the car. The tree that had fallen on the garage and allowed their escape was still lying across the driveway, and I had to park in the street. I didn't want to risk ruining the happy ending with a last-minute disaster. Not that there was much chance they would head anywhere but straight into the arms of the two little boys, about eight and ten years old, who ran down the driveway to greet us, their parents standing at the front door.

Amid a flurry of fur and smiles we were welcomed with cries of, "You found them, Delilah. Thank you, thank you," "Where have you been, kids?" and "How much do we owe you?"

I assured them my bill would be in the mail the next day, warning that it would include shelter impounds and traveling expenses. Other businesses may demand cash on delivery, but in my line of work getting the dogs home is (almost) its own reward. Anyway, if I held out for payment, I might be stuck with caring for pets for several days, or at least overnight. That's why usually, once a pet is located, I prefer to send the owner to pick it up. In the case of Matt and Matilda, however, there had been no point in leaving them to languish another day so far from home.

By the time we had dropped off the Malamutes, both Watson and I were beginning to droop, but we still had to pick up Trixie from Dr. Willie's, and when we got home, it was quite dark. I fed the dogs and opened a tin of British Heinz tomato soup for myself. The steak-and-kidney pie I put in the freezer for another day.

I played back my messages. The first was from Joe, saying my wagon was ready. I would return the minivan to Clyde's Renta Clunka first thing in the morning.

Beep. "Delilah." Joan Anderson's voice. *"Thought you'd like to know we found a wonderful new home for the Burmese. Thanks again for your help."*

Another happy ending! That's one that won't end up as coyote grub, I thought, pleased to have played a part in the cat's rescue.

Beep. "I'm having trouble with opossums invading my yard," a woman's voice said. *"Do mothballs help?"*

"Only if she has a good aim," I said, smiling at Watson and Trixie, who were listening in, Trixie perched on the desk with her head cocked, in a fair impersonation of the old RCA Victor "His Master's Voice" logo.

Beep. "Dee, are you there? Do pick up, there's a sweetie." Evie's voice hesitated, waiting for me to answer, then continued. *"I take it you're not there. It really is inconsiderate of you to never answer your phone, you know. Anyway, I just wanted to let you know that I will be popping in to see you the day after tomorrow. Be sure to be home."*

She didn't mention what time she might be popping in. It was typical of Evie to expect me to stay home all day, with bated breath, waiting for her to arrive. I would do my best, but if I had to go out, she would find a note on the door.

Beep. A woman's voice. *"I need to find a new home for my two Yorkies. I've had them for ten years, since they were puppies. But now I'm moving and my new place doesn't allow pets. They're well trained and lovable. I'm sure someone will give them a good home. I'm moving at the end of the week."*

There's someone who plans ahead. "If they're so well trained and lovable, why give them up?" I said aloud, addressing the caller.

Watson looked solemn.

"You'd better try a bit harder to find a place that accepts pets," I carried on. "And if you're so sure someone is out there just dying to adopt two ten-year-old dogs, their vet bills, and the behaviour problems that are bound to develop after being separated from the only home they've ever known, be my guest. Ten years, and she's giving them up!" I looked at Watson. "I'd live in a tent first."

Such calls made me so cross. Pets are like children. They are totally dependent upon us. Would she give up a child because of a no-children policy? Next time she'd better get one of those virtual reality pets I'd seen in the electronic stores.

Before going to bed, I took Watson and Trixie outside for one last tinkle. I kept the doggie door latched when Trixie stayed with us, and always went outside with her. I didn't trust her not to escape during the night and take off in search of Tony.

The wind was still blowing strong, carrying with it the sounds of the high-school marching band encouraging the football team to victory a few blocks away.

Tired as I was, something clicked in my mind, and I finally knew what had been bothering me ever since the Lizzie Walker case had begun.

Mavis Byrde was lying.

19

Cat's in the Cupboard

THE WIND WAS still blowing the next morning, snapping the red-and-yellow chevron-shaped flags that outlined the Renta Clunka lot. I parked the minivan and made my way to the single-storey office building, past the cars, trucks, and a rather smart motor home that made up Clyde's inventory.

I hoped the transaction wouldn't take long. I'd taken a chance and left Watson and Trixie at home alone. Watson would have been no trouble at all to bring along, but Trixie was a trial at the best of times. I would rather not have her underfoot while I dropped off one vehicle and picked up another, especially as Clyde would be accompanying me to Joe's garage to collect the wagon.

With the door and windows closed, the small office was stifling. There was no air-conditioning: beach cities seldom needed it; the current heat wave was an exception to our usually temperate, near-perfect climate. The office walls were bare except for a calendar from a local bank and a framed certificate showing that Clyde Ingram was a member of the Surf City Chamber of Commerce.

"Can't leave the door oben. Too widdy," explained Clyde as he hastily closed it behind me when I entered. "Widd blows the paperwork every which way."

He held a box of tissues in one hand, and I could see from his red and watery eyes that his allergies were still bothering him.

Business appeared to be brisk. Each time he started to reach into a pending tray for my paperwork, the telephone would ring, and he'd have to excuse himself.

"Looks like you could use some help," I said, eyeing the empty chair at the computer.

"Debbie, my girl, is ob vacation," he explained, his voice affected by his troubled sinuses. "Sorry about this," he went on as he pushed past me to reach a filing cabinet. "Be glad when we bove to larger quarters."

"Oh, you're moving? When?"

"Nothing's settled, but I'm pladding to expand the business soon, getting into used cars. I'm waiting for an investment to come through."

"Out of town?" I asked.

"No. We're waiting on the auto mart over on Parkside to be developed. It'll be perfect. Those old places have to bake way for progress."

He was talking about the early pioneer homes I had admired in Mavis's neighbourhood, so he wasn't going to get any sympathy from me. But I knew better than to enter into a preservation vs. development debate with a businessman.

The telephone rang again. Clyde's voice made me think the call was personal, and in an effort to give him some privacy, I moved out of the main office to a small adjoining alcove. It gave onto a bathroom and what I guessed to be a storage closet. I passed the time by washing my hands. The water was still running when I fancied that I heard a cat crying. Imagination, I told myself, a noise in the plumbing. But my ears were now on alert, and soon I heard the plaintive cry again.

I opened the closet door. Immediately a shorthaired red cat jumped out, then stood hesitating, unsure which way to go.

"Here, kitty," I said quietly.

The cat looked up at me with large green eyes, the eyes of an Abyssinian, if ever I saw one.

"Meowzart?" I queried, not expecting much in the way of a response. In my experience cats really don't care what you call them. They'll come if they feel like, especially if the call is accompanied by the rattle of a dinner dish. But to my surprise the cat did seem to recognize his name, and started to rub himself around my legs.

At that moment I heard Clyde complete his phone call, and the next moment he was looking into the alcove for me.

"What the . . . ?" he exclaimed. "Where did that cat come from?"

"I found him in your closet. Is it yours?"

"Of course it's not mine. I hate cats. Get it out of here. No wonder I haven't been able to breathe properly all week." He groped in his pocket, brought out a small vial from which he extracted a tablet, placing it on his tongue. Then he made as if to open the office door and shush the cat outside.

I quickly stood in his way. ''It's all right if I take it, then? I think it might belong to a client of mine who lost one just like this several days ago.''

''I don't care what you do with it. Just get it out of here.'' He started to sneeze again, more violently than ever.

''Well, you can't blame the cat,'' I said defensively. ''He didn't ask to be shut in your closet.''

''How the hell did it get in there?'' he demanded, when the fit of sneezing had subsided.

''Perhaps it came in one of your rentals,'' I said. ''Cats love to get into cars and can be transported miles before escaping.''

Was that what had happened to Meowzart? Maybe one of Clyde's rentals had been in Mavis's neighbourhood when the cat ran off. Or maybe Clyde himself? Come to think of it, if I had heard Estelle correctly when she drove off yesterday, there may have been a reason he was in the area.

''Could you hold him a minute while I go and get a carrier out of the van?'' I asked, a little unkindly.

''No way I'm holding that thing. Cats. They're devils!'' he said with a shudder.

I thought that was a little strong, but then I wasn't besieged by allergies. Even so, I considered his aversion to cats to go beyond a mere physical allergy to cat hair and dander. It almost bordered on ailurophobia, an actual fear of cats.

I took Meowzart out to the minivan and placed him in a carrier. Unconfined cats do not make good driving companions. Meowzart would be sure to bolt at the first opportunity, and I knew Clyde wouldn't be much help. Fortunately, in my haste to get going that morning, I had forgotten to unload my gear before returning the van.

Clyde was extremely annoyed when it became apparent that the cat was coming with us. He was, however, obliged to drive me to pick up my wagon, sneezing and cursing the cat all the way. Luckily for us all, it was no more than a ten-minute drive to Joe's garage, where Clyde unceremoniously dumped me and my cat carrier and other gear out on the sidewalk.

Joe was a lot easier to get along with than Clyde. The only negative thing he had to say that morning was that it was time I replaced my station wagon with something more reliable.

"I don't know how much more I can patch it up for you, Delilah, before it starts costing you more money than it's worth," he said as he helped me reload the wagon.

"Nothing I'd like better," I said, though secretly I was rather attached to the old banger. "But it'll have to wait until I win the lottery."

Business would have to get a lot better before I could begin to think about new cars. But things were looking up. Two cases completed in two days. For although he wore no ID tag and had no distinguishing marks, I was positive that the cat now carrying on like he was being put through a wringer was Meowzart.

The only question was, how did he get into Clyde's closet? It certainly wasn't by invitation.

20

The Prodigal Returns

"DELILAH! YOU FOUND him. Just in time for the show. How wonderful!"

It was later the same morning. I had driven to Mavis's house immediately after picking up my station wagon.

Mavis, still in her negligee, this time a diaphanous green affair, her long blonde hair hanging loose around her shoulders, had rushed out the front door with outstretched arms when she saw me drive up.

"Come to Mommy, you naughty little puss cat," she cooed, lifting the runaway from the cat carrier. "Were you frightened? You poor thing. Never mind. Mommy's here now. Let me look at you.

"Delilah, do come in." She gestured me to enter, almost as an afterthought.

Placing Meowzart on top of the grand piano that dominated the spacious living room, she continued to check him over.

"I hope you didn't pick up any fleas," she said, running her hands through his fur. "Let me look at your poor little tootsies. Did you have to walk very far?"

Continuing in this vein, she peered at the cat's eyes, mouth, and ears, cleaning him with the edge of her negligee.

"My, you're so thin. We'll have to fatten you up for the show. Come along to the kitchen, darling. I've been saving a yummy piece of smoked salmon just for you."

Meowzart jumped down from the piano and followed her out of the room.

"I won't be a minute, Delilah," she trilled. "But I really must get some nourishment into the poor thing."

Actually I thought Meowzart looked pretty good considering he hadn't eaten for several days. He had been very thirsty, of course, and I had given him water from my cooler as soon as I got back to the station wagon. But my guess was he'd had plenty of reserves to last him through his ordeal.

The spacious living room was decorated in a style one might expect of Mavis, reflective of her taste in clothes and her twin passions of music and cats. Flounced white muslin draperies hung at the huge picture window which gave onto the fair prospect of a well-tended front yard. Porcelain figures of cats playing on, or actually playing, pianos, stood on every available ledge and end table. One wall was given over entirely to cat show rosettes, photos of Abbys, and a trophy case. On the square glass coffee table a huge chintz-and-ribbon-covered scrapbook lay open invitingly at what would be, I ventured to guess, a significant event in Mavis's concert career.

Over the mantel hung an oil painting depicting an idealized Mavis in a moment of glory on the concert stage.

She was dressed in an electric-blue ball gown, a glittering tiara on her expertly coiffed hair. One gloved hand rested delicately on the pianoforte, the other held a bouquet of flowers. More flowers lay at her feet. Was there ever really such a moment, I wondered, or was this an extravagant indulgence? I stifled the uncharitable thought. We had all, had we not, seen better days. At least Mavis, from the looks of things, had managed to acquire considerable resources one way or another. More power to her, I thought, comparing her comfort with my own modest means.

On a sunny spot on the red brocade couch, Meowzart's kitty kin, Pussini and Depussy, washed each other behind the ears. Whispering, perhaps, something spiteful about the prodigal Meowzart being rewarded with smoked salmon.

Mavis came back into the room. "Now, Delilah, how much do I owe you?"

Since she was well-off, I would have liked to pad the bill a little. She could afford it, and it was my way of subsidizing senior citizens like Mrs. Jones, whose poodle was always running off. But since serendipity had, on this occasion, played such a very large part in Meowzart's recovery, I really didn't feel I could justify such an act.

"I haven't had time to prepare the bill yet," I said. "I'll mail it to you."

"Delilah, he's so thin. It looks like he hasn't eaten for days. Where did you find him?" she asked.

"It was really odd," I said. "I was returning a rental

car, and while I was at the agency I heard a cat crying. I opened a closet door, and there he was.''

Mavis paled. ''Oh my. Locked in a closet, the poor angel. He might have starved to death.''

Another thought seemed to occur to her. ''A car rental agency, you said?''

''Yes. Renta Clunka down on Main Street.''

Her hand fluttered to her throat. ''Clyde Ingram's?''

''Yes. Do you know him?''

Her never-still hands patted the back of her hair. ''We go out occasionally.'' She smiled coyly.

''That explains it, then,'' I said. ''I wondered how Meowzart got there. He probably hitched a ride in Clyde's car.''

''Oh, I don't think so. Clyde never visits me here. He's allergic to cats, you know.''

''So I've noticed,'' I said dryly.

''Sometimes''—she giggled—''he seems to be allergic even to me. I suppose I must have cat hair or dander clinging to my clothes.''

I smiled at the image of Mavis and Clyde, their dalliances interrupted by heavy bouts of sneezing.

Mavis chose to ignore the smile. ''Yes. We always meet elsewhere. As a matter of fact . . .'' Her voice trailed off, as if she had been about to say something, but had thought better of it.

''Well, if you'll excuse me, I have to give Meowzart a bath, start getting him in shape for the show. Have you ever been to a cat show, Delilah? Do come. I can get you a pass. This is a biggie, an international event.

Meowzart will be competing against the best in the world. Cats from Japan, Europe, Australia, and Canada. It's a very important occasion for us. The competition is fierce. And the jealousy! Would you believe one woman has threatened to burn my house down if Meowzart wins the Grand Premier competition. You know, I was beginning to think *she* might have stolen him."

I was intrigued by the idea that a cat contest could arouse such passions, and I told her I'd think about attending.

Actually I had something else on my mind. Suspecting that she had not been entirely truthful about what she'd heard the night of the murder, I had been going to ask for more details. But the words died in my mouth as she spoke.

"Don't forget to send me your bill," she said. "Of course, since you found Meowzart by accident, I won't expect to pay more than the minimum fee."

I could have told her that but for me, her boyfriend would have kicked her precious cat out into the street. But I decided to bide my time until I had all the facts in what was starting to look like a very interesting, albeit at this point purely hypothethical, scenario.

"Do be sure to pick up some ID tags and breakaway collars next time you're at the pet store," I said as Mavis showed me to the door. "For just a few dollars you can save yourself a lot of heartache, not to mention inconvenience."

Inconvenience wasn't the half of it. If I was right,

Mavis Byrde was going to regret the day she decided to call me in.

As I made my way back to my station wagon, I noticed Detective Mallory's car in Lizzie Walker's driveway next door. He was just arriving. In grey slacks, a light blue shirt, tie loosened at the neck, navy-blue blazer slung over his shoulder, he looked more like someone on a social call than a police detective reviewing a crime scene.

"Hello, Mrs. Doolittle," he called, catching sight of me as he walked up the path to Lizzie's front door.

I waved back, suddenly conscious that my white jeans and pink T-shirt were covered in cat hair. However, mindful of his oft-repeated accusations that I interfered with his investigations, I approached the white picket fence separating the two yards, prepared to explain my presence there and to offer proof that I really had been looking for a lost cat when I had discovered Lizzie's body.

Also, not incidentally, though this was a little harder for me to explain to myself, it was important to me that he know I could be successful at my job.

"I've just returned Ms. Byrde's cat. I found it this morning," I said somewhat smugly.

"Congratulations. You solved your case. I wish mine was as easy," he replied with a smile.

I ignored the implication that pet detecting was a breeze. His words gave me the opening I'd been looking for.

"It's strange how it happened. The cat must have got into somebody's car and been taken for a ride."

"Interesting," he said, rather too politely to be sincere.

I refused to be discouraged. "Yes. Actually, I was lucky. I found the cat at Renta Clunka, the car rental place."

His blue-grey eyes narrowed. At last I seemed to have caught his interest.

"What were you doing there?"

"My car broke down, so I was obliged to rent one. Renta Clunka offered the most reasonable rates. Anyway," I went on, "the cat had managed to get itself shut in a closet. Clyde Ingram, the owner, had no idea how the cat got there, but as I explained to him, cats often get into cars for warmth or protection, and then find themselves transported miles from home."

"Did you tell him it was Ms. Byrde's cat?" he asked.

"I don't believe I mentioned her name. I didn't even know they were acquainted until just now, when Mavis told me." I hesitated before offering him my theory, then went on, "Since the cat went missing about the same time as Lizzie Walker was killed, maybe the murderer used a rental car. Do you think it's worth checking out?"

His reaction, though not what I had hoped for was, upon reflection, no more than I might have expected.

"Mrs. Doolittle," he said, running his hand through his unruly grey hair. "I don't meddle in your business. I wish you'd stay out of mine. How do you even know if it's the same cat? They all look alike to me. Just because some stray cat shows up in a place of business across town—''

Recovering from this verbal assault with what I considered well-bred presence of mind, I interrupted. ''It's not some stray cat. It's an Abyssinian.''

''I don't care if it's a bloody Martian,'' he exclaimed, clearly exasperated.

That's all the thanks I got for offering him a perfectly excellent lead, one which I was quite sure he would never have come across on his own.

He seemed to have a talent for bringing out the worst in me. ''Well,'' I said huffily, ''it's quite obvious you know nothing about cats.''

Any regrets I might have been harbouring about not informing him of Estelle's secret life and her false alibi, or about my suspicion that Mavis Byrde was lying about the events of the night of the murder, vanished in the resentment I felt at that moment.

Estelle had promised to come forward in a day or two. Detective Jack Mallory, Surf City Police Department, Homicide Division, could jolly well wait until then.

21
A Hiss of Cats

HALLOWEEN AFTERNOON FOUND me at the World Cat Show held every October at the County Convention Center, where an amazing number of cat lovers were willing to fork over six dollars for parking, plus another five for admission, to see something they could see for nothing any day of the week at the local shelter.

But on second thought, probably not cats like these. Almost a thousand examples of feline excellence, pampered and groomed within an inch of their lives.

"How about a cat show?" I had asked Evie, who, back from her trip up north, was staying with me for a few days while Howard took care of some business in Los Angeles.

"I'm just a teensy bit bored with shopping, darling," she had complained. "When one has done Paris, London, and New York all in the last six months, what else is there?"

What indeed?

Tony was enlisted to care for the dogs in our absence.

He was delighted to oblige, and spend some time with Trixie.

Sharing Sam's cramped apartment was not going well for him.

"It's them snakes of 'is. They don't 'arf pong," Tony said, holding his nose.

Though Sam had been released from jail, he was still a suspect, confirming my suspicion that Estelle had not yet been to the police to verify his alibi.

"Cats! Got no time for 'em," Tony had snorted on learning where we were going.

"Well, in that case you won't mind staying behind and taking care of the dogs," I said.

"Suits me," he had replied.

Some folks are decidedly dog people or cat people, each ready to extol the virtues of their preference, often at the expense of the other. Dog people citing loyalty and companionship. Cat people countering with gentleness and self-reliance.

My own conclusion, reached after years of both cat and dog ownership, was that there are two main differences—language comprehension and conscience. Dogs have both. Cats have neither.

Even a poorly trained dog will soon learn a number of words: *no, dinner, walkies, cookie, ball, sit,* and so forth. A cat will respond only to his name, and not even then unless it is uttered in conjunction with the sounds of food preparation.

But the most notable distinction between dogs and

cats is guilt. Dogs seem to be born with it; cats don't know the meaning of the word.

Scold a dog and he'll grovel at your feet. But a cat will kill your pet parakeet and merely blink and walk away with maddening indifference.

It had not been easy to persuade Evie to leave Chamois behind. But dogs were definitely persona non grata at cat shows, and even though the little Maltese was usually quiet as a mouse inside his sport bag, one never knew what might set off an involuntary yapping.

Fussing like an anxious mother leaving her newborn baby, Evie instructed Tony regarding Chamois's care.

"Please grill this lamb chop for his dinner," she said, reaching into the refrigerator. "And be sure to take the meat off the bone before you give it to him."

As she turned to put the chop back into the refrigerator, Tony gave me a wink, licked his lips, and rubbed his stomach. There would be no lamb chop for Chamois that evening.

"Now, dear boy, you must remember to put him outside as soon as he's eaten," Evie continued. "And wipe his paws when he comes in. I don't want him to pick up any infection from the grass."

"Anything you say, luv. Do you want me to wipe his little bum while I'm at it?"

Ignoring, or perhaps unaware of, the sarcasm, she replied, "Well, if you wouldn't mind . . ."

"Don't worry about a thing, luv," he reassured her. "I'll take good care of the little bloke."

"And for heaven's sake, don't forget to give him his pill before he goes down for his nap."

Tony rolled his eyes. "Yes, luv," he said seriously.

AT THE CAT show Evie and I made our way through the crowds past aisles of cages, each row devoted to a different breed. The word *cages* really didn't do justice to the exotic compartments draped in brocades, velvets, and silks, in which the feline elite lay on fancy cushions or canopy beds. The only indication that these were, after all, only cats, was that great leveler, the kitty-litter box in the corner of each cage.

Concern for the health of the cats was expressed in the warning that hung on every cage door: PLEASE KEEP FINGERS OUT OF THE CAGE. YOUR AFFECTION MAY SPREAD INFECTION.

"Sounds like a slogan for safe sex," said Evie, who had been about to pet a particularly handsome Somali.

"Do look at these adorable creatures," she said, halting beside a litter of cream-coloured Persian bundles of furry joy. "You know, I really do think I might like to get a kitten."

"If you have time to groom it every day. Persians are high-maintenance animals. Get a shorthair, if you must. Better yet," I said, "let's go to the shelter. They've got everything there—most breeds, any colour, any sex you want."

"But not purebred kittens?" she countered.

"Sometimes. But anyway, they're kittens for such a short time, what difference does it make?"

I thought of the Burmese I had recently trapped at the feral cat colony. Had he started out as a high-priced kitten like those now being offered for five, six, seven hundred dollars and more?

"How do they come by these names?" Evie was saying. "Did they really originate in Siam, Burma, Persia, Somalia, or wherever?"

"I have no idea. Maybe some did. More likely the breeders were simply looking for something exotic sounding."

"What's the difference between an American and a British shorthair? A Devon and a Cornish Rex?"

The distinctions seemed to me too fine for all but the most devoted auriophile to care about. As far as I was concerned, the fanciest, tiara-topped cat in the show was not that far removed from the wildest tiger, the genetic changes being only cosmetic.

"The Norwegian forest cat is the only one I know to be a truly original species, descended from the wild cats of Norway," I said, pausing to admire the huge double-coated cats housed in a splendid glass-and-wood cage, shaped and decorated like a Viking ship.

A cat show is a great place for people-watching, too. Shorts and cat-decorated T-shirts were the uniform of the day, leopard-print and tiger-stripe fabrics predominating.

I felt overdressed in my tan cotton pants suit and cream silk shirt. I had made an effort for Evie's sake. She was a standout in a tailored white linen three-piece, the sleeveless blouse showing off her polished tan. The hat she had selected for this occasion was a gold straw boater. White high-heeled sandals revealed tanned, coral-tipped toes. I'd had the foresight to wear comfortable shoes, but Evie had refused to spoil the effect by donning flats.

"I say there. What frightful manners," she cried. Her clarion tones were loud enough to be heard by all within earshot except the rather large woman to whom they were directed. In leopard-print spandex tights, topped by a voluminous chartreuse smock, she carried a plate of nachos, and was clearly in a hurry, barely missing dabbing Evie's white suit with melted cheese and salsa as she pushed past us.

Fortunately the vendor booths provided a distraction.

"You didn't tell me there'd be shopping," said Evie, delighted to discover a new outlet for her passion.

Anything that might appeal to the showgoer, as long as it was embellished with a picture of a cat, preferably a specific breed, was there for the buying—from mugs and stationery, to T-shirts, tights, jackets, and dresses. Evie lingered at the jewelry booth, where she was rather taken with a three-thousand-dollar gold necklace of cats with emerald eyes.

At the cat-furnishings booth I wondered idly what Hobo might make of the five-hundred-dollar cat tree, so elaborate it would take up my entire sitting room. I settled for a bottle of vitamins and a pot of grow-your-own cat grasses at the cat health-food bar.

Around the perimeter of the huge convention hall were the judging rings. Not rings exactly, they were large booths, with a table for the judge, cages for the contestants arranged along the back, and a dozen or so chairs for the spectators. Several judgings took place at the same time, and the more successful contestants progressed from one ring to another as they advanced through the competition.

There were cat seminars given by experts. At one end of the hall I recognized Dr. Veronica Veracruz, a noted cat veterinarian, who was giving a talk on the merits of early spaying or neutering. I was afraid it would fall on deaf ears in this crowd of breed fanciers.

Later a representative from a well-known pet food company was to present a seminar on nutrition. Pet care was a billion-dollar industry. It was a constant source of amazement to me that people would lavish so much money on pets on the one hand, yet on the other be so quick to dispose of them as soon as they became an inconvenience.

We located Mavis with the other Abyssinian breeders. She was resplendent in a frilly long-sleeved cream-coloured muslin blouse and tiered skirt, her blonde hair caught up in purple ribbons on top of her head ("Purple for good luck," she told us).

She barely waited for an introduction to Evie before bursting out, "We won, we won! Meowzart has taken Grand Premier Cat." She almost dropped the huge purple ribbon rosette in her excitement.

"Congratulations," we both murmured, trying to look suitably impressed.

I left Evie and Mavis talking kittens, and made my

way to Estelle's booth, just across the aisle. She was once again in the trappings of mysticism, quite unrecognizable from the lemonade-dispensing grandmother I had met in Winona a few days earlier.

''How's it going?'' I greeted her.

She shrugged; business was slow, she said, blaming it on the location of her booth. Situated as she was next to the information desk, her voice was frequently drowned out by the public-address system giving instructions to competitors to take their cats to the various judging rings.

To my hurried, ''Did you speak to the police?'' she answered, ''Not yet. Tomorrow, after the show's over, I promise.''

''You must,'' I urged, ''and soon. Sam Vyper is still under suspicion.''

To one side of her booth stood an easel holding a poster. COMMUNICATE WITH YOUR CAT. ANIMAL CLAIRVOYANCE. BRING ME YOUR CAT'S PICTURE, it said.

Intrigued, I rummaged in my purse for the snapshot of Hobo I'd been carrying around intending to show to Dr. Willie. In the photo, the big orange cat was sitting on my back porch idly contemplating the bird feeder hanging just out of his reach.

Estelle looked at the picture and said, ''He loves to be outdoors, especially on the wetlands.''

Well, I thought, ever the skeptic, that could apply to most cats in our area.

''He has a friend,'' she went on. ''A big red dog. And

there's a little white dog he doesn't like at all. And he's worried about the latched doggie door.''

Extraordinary. Maybe she was a witch after all. Or maybe she just had a keen ear for gossip.

Across the aisle, Mavis, explaining the finer points of Abbys and Somalis to Evie, had moved away from Meowzart's cage to point out the Somalis on the next aisle. Suddenly I saw the nacho woman, who had been strolling nonchalantly in our direction, reach into Meowzart's cage, grab him, tuck him under her flowing smock, and start walking away, her pace quickening as she neared the exit.

I had to act quickly, but the crowds were too dense for me to stop the woman before she reached the exit. I dashed across the few feet between Estelle's booth and the information desk, reached across the counter, and snatched the microphone from the hand of a startled young man who had been in the midst of saying, ''Last call for Japanese bobtail kittens to ring number nine.''

''Loose cat,'' I cried over the public-address system. ''There is a cat loose.''

The only thing likely to add more suspense to a cat show than who's going to take home the Grand Premier award is the cry ''loose cat.'' Security is tightened; exit doors slam shut, and nothing short of an earthquake will open them until the cat is captured.

The lights dimmed, then went up again and an official voice said, ''Ladies and gentlemen, a cat has escaped. Please remain where you are, quite still, until the owner can capture him.''

I headed for the nearest security guard and told him what I had observed. I had spotted the woman making her way to the rest room. Her story, when apprehended, that she had merely wanted to inspect the cat more closely, was accepted by everyone except poor Mavis, who barely had time to realize that Meowzart was missing before I returned him to her.

"That's her," Mavis said. Her voice trembling with indignation, she pointed at the would-be cat napper now heading for the exit. "The woman I told you about, who threatened to burn down my house if Meowzart won."

Poor Mavis's troubles were not over.

Later, while snacking on overpriced lattes and croissants at one of the food booths and listening to Evie lecture—"Delilah, you really are the limit. We can't even come to a cat show without you causing a scene"—a loud "A-choo!" caused me to glance toward the entrance.

Clyde Ingram! What in the world would possess him to come to a cat show?

As Evie leafed through the program, commenting on the various merits of Abbys and Somalis, my eyes followed Clyde, looking a little out of place in a dark blue business suit as he made his way to Mavis's side. His progress was halted every few seconds as he stopped to sneeze, placing his hand over his mouth in a futile attempt to stave off the cat hair and dander that filled the air.

Mavis and Clyde were soon engaged in a heated conversation, both of them from time to time glancing in

Estelle's direction, as if concerned she might overhear. It looked as though he was trying to persuade her about something, at one point taking her hand in his, then almost immediately removing it again to cover another sneeze, considerably hampering his powers of persuasion, I would guess. Mavis shook her head a couple of times, but finally appeared to relent, for he gave her a quick hug and left, staggering with sneezes as he made his way back to the exit.

Glancing in the direction of Estelle's booth, I was surprised to see that she was packing up to leave.

22
Evening Callers

"I CAN'T WAIT to get my shoes off," said Evie, easing her feet out of her high heels.

The October evenings were closing in, and it was dark by the time we arrived home. Tony had drawn the curtains and turned on the lights, and my little house offered a welcoming haven as we pulled into the driveway.

"I'm gasping for a cup of tea," I said. "I hope Tony has put the kettle on." He had, and before long we were comfortably settled in the sitting room with a tea tray and, I was surprised to see, a plate of biscuits.

Chamois and Watson had greeted us with wagging tails.

"Come here, my treasure," said Evie, picking up the little Maltese and planting a lipsticky kiss on his already pink head. But he wriggled out of Evie's arms and ran over to Tony. Lamb chop or no, Chamois had found a new friend.

"Them cookies is all right," said Tony. "Went over the top a bit, though, didn't you, making them in the shape of dog bones?"

"You ate the dog biscuits?" I said. It was an accusation as much as a question.

Tony's face dropped. "Dog biscuits! Blimey! I *thought* they could do with a bit more sugar."

"I made them for the shelter's open house next week. I don't have time to bake more. You'll just have to give a donation instead."

"You might 'ave warned me," he grumbled good-naturedly.

"They won't do you any harm," I countered. "Probably more wholesome than half the junk food you eat."

He shrugged and changed the subject. "How was the show?"

"More exciting than one might have expected," said Evie, settling into a corner of the couch and plumping up a cushion behind her back. She inserted a Sobranie cigarette into a long gold holder, flicked a tiny gold lighter with elegantly manicured nails, then proceeded to tell Tony how Mavis had almost lost Meowzart.

"Well I'm blowed," said Tony. "And Delilah, 'ere, saved the day? Well played, Mrs. D."

He got to his feet. "Better be off. See how old Slippery's getting on. Poor sod. He's right down in the dumps over this Lizzie Walker business."

"I hope it won't be for much longer," I said.

"What d'you mean?" he asked.

"Estelle LaBelle was at the show. She told me she intends to go to the police tomorrow, to tell them that she did indeed hire Sam to clean up Lizzie's backyard."

"Why would she do that? Hire Sam, I mean. What's

Lizzie Walker got to do with 'er?'' Tony sat down again, his expression a mixture of curiosity and concern.

An explanation was necessary. I had said too much to stop now. ''I suppose it's all right to tell you. It will come out eventually.''

''Do tell,'' said Evie. ''I love a bit of scandal.''

''Apparently Estelle is Lizzie's daughter,'' I said.

''Get away,'' said Tony. ''First I've 'eard of it.''

''First anyone's heard of it,'' I said. ''Estelle has kept it a secret for years.''

''Why?''

''She has her reasons. I really don't feel at liberty to say more.''

''Oh no,'' said Evie. ''You're not going to get away with that.'' She took another puff of her cigarette, delicately removed a piece of tobacco from the corner of her mouth, and commanded, ''Tell all.''

I really didn't need much encouragment. The whole story was weighing heavily on my mind, and I find that it helps to talk things through, especially when I'm trying to solve a puzzle.

''Well, apparently, Estelle ran away from home as a teenager. She got pregnant,'' I explained.

''In the club, was she?'' Tony nodded sagely.

''How is it that you're so well-informed?'' asked Evie, reaching for the teapot and pouring herself another cup.

I told them about my trip to Winona and what I'd learned of Estelle's double life. ''The night her mother was killed, when she told the police she was at the pictures, she had, in fact, been visiting her daughter. She was still trying to keep her relationship with Lizzie a secret."

"So that's why she kept quiet about Sam," said Tony.

I nodded. "She didn't know he'd been accused of Lizzie's murder until I told her. Then she begged me to give her time to tell her family before she went to the police, which, as I said, she's promised to do tomorrow."

"Well, that's a relief," said Tony.

"But what about the father of the child? The teenage sweetheart?" asked Evie.

"She never said, and I didn't ask. I don't know that it matters anyway, at this late date."

Our cosy teatime was interrupted by a loud rapping on the front door, sending the three dogs into a barking frenzy, ready to repel all invaders. Watson, with ears erect, stood on alert behind Trixie, who pawed frantically at the door. Chamois, preparing for a rearguard action, barked from a safe distance under the coffee table.

Grabbing hold of Trixie's collar, I opened the door to Officer Offley and Detective Mallory. They declined my invitation to enter, choosing to conduct their business on the porch, behind the screen door, apparently put off by the canine greeting committee.

Mallory peered through the screen into the sitting room, cast a suspicious glance in Tony's direction, then said, "Mrs. Doolittle, we're following up on the statement you made after you discovered the body of Mrs. Elizabeth Walker."

"Yes?" I said inquiringly.

"You said you saw a makeshift altar, on which stood a candlestick and a photograph. Can you give us any more details about the photograph?"

"I don't think so. As I said in my statement, it appeared to be of a family—a mother, father, and two children."

"Did you recognize anyone in the photograph?"

"No, I didn't."

"You're quite sure it was there? You didn't imagine it?"

"Well, of course I'm sure. Why in the world would I make up something like that? Why do you ask?" Every detail of that terrible scene was etched in my memory. I would never forget it, and there's no way I would have imagined a thing.

"And you didn't take anything?" persisted Mallory.

Tony, who until then had been sitting quietly, taking it all in, got to his feet. " 'Ere, hang about a bit, mate," he said. "Are you accusing Mrs. D of stealing evidence?"

"Don't say another word, Dee!" Evie's cut-glass tones rang out from the couch. "I'm calling Howard straightaway and have him get in touch with Max, our attorney, immediately. This is harassment, pure and simple, and we shall sue."

She got to her feet and joined Tony at the door. All this time Trixie and Chamois had kept up an incesssant yapping, while Watson waited only for the command "Seize 'im."

We must have made an intimidating crowd.

Mallory consulted his notebook, then said, "Thank you. I won't keep you from your guests any longer. I'll add this to your statement."

Offley had already headed back down the driveway when Mallory, appearing to have second thoughts, lowered his voice and added, "Mrs. Doolittle, would you mind stepping outside. I'd like a word with you in private."

Puzzling over what he might have to say that couldn't have been said just as easily in front of my guests, and using my foot to prevent Trixie from escaping, I eased my way out on to the porch.

"I followed up on your suggestion about Clyde Ingram," Mallory said. "He told me he was out of town the night of the murder. Traveling in his motor home with a friend. Not an easy alibi to confirm."

I nodded, mildly flattered that he had confided in me. Realizing that I'd not been entirely forthcoming with him, I regretted my promise to Estelle that I'd give her time to go to the police. "And I'd advise you not to tell anyone else about the photograph," Mallory continued. "We don't know if it has any significance or not, but until the case is closed, your knowledge could put you at risk." He grasped my arm as he spoke, as if to emphasize the urgency of his words.

It was a caution he would be duty-bound to offer anyone in similar circumstances. I had no reason to believe he was prompted by personal concern for my welfare, and I was annoyed that such a thought even entered my head.

Before I had a chance to reply, he turned abruptly and followed Offley to the black and white police car waiting at the curb.

Tony and Evie eyed me curiously as I went back indoors. Evie's gaze seemed particularly penetrating, and I felt a little flustered remembering her earlier remarks about my being attracted to the detective.

But for once she refrained from comment, saying only, "Of all the bloody cheek! He all but accused you of murder!"

"Calm down. He's only doing his job," I said.

"That's the first I've heard about there being an altar," said Tony. "Is them rumours true, then? Was the old dear really into witchcraft?"

"If she was," I replied, "it was all perfectly harmless, I'm sure. From what I knew of her, the poor woman barely had her wits about her. I don't think she was capable of doing much damage."

"Could run in the family, though, don't you think?" said Tony.

"What do you mean?"

"Well, there's Estelle, the psychic palm reader. You just got through telling us that she's Lizzie's daughter. Maybe they were both part of some secret cult that's been responsible for the cat killings."

"Or maybe," put in Evie, "somebody wants you to think that they were."

Tony and I looked at her in amazement. It had taken someone from outside our tight-knit community to come up with a different perspective on things.

"Why are you looking at me like that? What did I say?" she said, smiling. "Hadn't that occurred to either of you? Darlings, if I've learned anything at all in this life, it is that things are seldom what they seem."

23

Searching for Answers

"GOING OUT? AT this hour? It's past eight o'clock!" Evie made no effort to hide her annoyance.

The theme from *Laura* wafted from the television. They don't make films like that anymore. Subtle, black-and-white, delicately nuanced.

Tony had left, and Evie and I had been all set for a cosy evening with a video of our all-time favourite picture.

I had made a fresh pot of tea and had taken the Dundee fruitcake that Great-Aunt Nell had sent me for Christmas out of the freezer. How had Tony missed it? I wondered, as I absentmindedly picked off a couple of the almonds arranged in concentric circles over the top and popped them in my mouth.

But much as I wanted to relax after the hectic day, I was too distracted. Mallory's visit had disturbed me more than I had let on to Evie and Tony. I was annoyed and, I had to admit, a little hurt, that he even entertained the idea that I took the photograph. I believed I held the key to solving the crime, but I hadn't yet been able to sort things through in my mind. I would not be able to settle down until I had solved the mystery of Lizzie Walker's murder.

I said: "There's somebody I need to see. You can come if you like." This last uttered in the certain knowledge that she wouldn't want to.

"Go if you must." She pouted. "But nothing in the world would induce me to put my shoes on again."

It was hard to think clearly with Evie carrying on about her aching feet and asking did I have a footbath. Even though I had assured her several times that I did not possess such a thing, she continued to rummage in the hall closet.

"These old photographs!" she declared, coming across a box of snapshots. "Why are you still hanging on to these pictures of Roger? No happy memories there."

I am one of those people who are congenitally unable to throw anything away—clothes that I will never again wear, collars and tags of pets long gone, and boxes of photographs that would never find their way into albums, but still held so much meaning that I couldn't just put them in the dustbin.

"Photographs," Evie was saying, "are nothing but ghosts from the past. Get rid of them. You must live in the present."

She was right. "I'll get around to it sooner or later," I said, taking the box from her and stuffing it back on the shelf behind the spare blankets and pillows. But even as I did so my mind made the connection that my subconscious had been seeking.

The photograph I had observed on Lizzie's pathetic little altar the day I discovered her body. The one Detective Mallory now claimed was missing. *Ghosts of the past,* Evie had said. Where were they now? Lizzie and Dennis were dead; Estelle was still here. And the little boy, Estelle's stepbrother? A grown man now, whose last name I'd had trouble hearing when Estelle said it at the Winona Tastee-Freez. It now echoed in my mind clear as the proverbial bell.

"Well, as long as you're going out," Evie said, "be a sweetie and stop by the chemist's and see if they have a footbath. Oh, and get me some ciggies, would you? I'm almost out."

The wind was still blowing hard, but the direction had changed and it was quite chilly out. I borrowed Evie's Liberty scarf to put around my head. I always felt a bit scruffy in a head scarf, but it was dark, I wasn't making any social calls, and well, if it was good enough for Queen Elizabeth on Derby Day, it was good enough for me.

"There's plenty of trick-or-treat candy for the children," I told Evie as I left. "It's in a basket by the front door. I hope you don't mind."

"What fun!" she said. "You know, living in a condo, we don't get the trick-or-treaters like we used to at the house. No, I won't mind at all." She helped me on with my coat. "But if those policemen come round again, I'll . . . I'll . . ." She hesitated, searching for a suitable retaliation for the law. ''I'll set the dogs on them!'' she finished.

''Well, you'll have to make do with Chamois and Trixie,'' I said. ''Watson's coming with me.''

24

Ghosts and Goblins

CLOUDS SCUDDED ACROSS a full moon, and the wind whipped at the costumes of the young ghosts and goblins who raced screeching along the streets, dropping their candy in their excitement, and I drove with extra caution as I made my way to Parkside.

Mavis was startled to see me standing at her door, as well she might be. Her hands full of candy, she had obviously been expecting trick-or-treaters.

"I won't come in," I said. "I've got my dog with me." Watson stood close to my side. Ears erect, muscles taut, she seemed to know that she was "on a case."

"Is it about your bill? I haven't had time to mail the check yet," she said.

"No. And I'm sorry to disturb you. I just have one quick question. It's about Lizzie Walker's murder, actually."

"I don't know anything more than what I've already told the police," she said nervously.

"It's to satisfy my own curiosity, really," I said. "I'm concerned that Estelle is being implicated in the crime because of your statement that you overheard her arguing with Lizzie the night of the murder. And I'm fairly sure that couldn't have been the case. Is there a possibility you might have been mistaken?''

I was quite prepared for her to slam the door in my face.

Instead she gave a nervous little giggle, patted the back of her head, and said, ''Yes. You're right. Silly me. I was mistaken. I realized it just this evening, after the show, when I was scheduling my piano students' lessons for next month. I have every intention of informing that delightful Detective Mallory tomorrow morning.''

I was about to thank her nicely and leave when she volunteered the information I had already guessed at.

''As a matter of fact''—she patted her hair again—''I was away for the weekend with a friend, in his motor home.''

''Clyde Ingram,'' I said. ''Is that what he was persuading you to say when I saw him talking with you at the cat show this afternoon?''

''I don't know what you mean.''

''I think you do. But perhaps you wouldn't be quite so quick to protect him if you knew how he treated Meowzart the day I found him at Renta Clunka.''

I proceeded to tell her how cruelly he had tried to kick poor Meowzart out the door, embroidering the story as much as my conscience would allow.

''I don't believe it,'' she cried, putting her hand to her throat.

''He's using you, Mavis, and you're up to your neck in a murder case.''

This time she did slam the door in my face.

25

Unmasked

"SOMEBODY'S BEEN TRYING to make the cat killings look like witchcraft," I said to Watson as we drove toward Main Street. "Who, you ask, and why? Good questions, my dear Watson. I think we're about to find out."

I had no idea if Clyde would still be in his office at this hour. But with his secretary on vacation, he might have had to stay late to catch up on paperwork.

"Mrs. Doolittle," he said when I entered his office. "Need to rent again? Maybe you should think about replacing your station wagon. I can get you into a nice little—"

"No," I interrupted. "I took a chance I might find you still here. I'm finishing up some paperwork myself, completing my case report on the lost cat—you remember?" I refreshed his memory. "The one I discovered in your closet the other day?"

He nodded, and looked as if he was about to sneeze again at the mere recollection.

"We pet detectives have to keep careful records, you

know, to justify our expense accounts. It's important that each case be thoroughly detailed.''

He was all politeness and affability.

''Sit down, little lady. Can I get you a cup of coffee?'' he said, turning to the electric coffee maker perched precariously on a narrow bookshelf.

I remained standing, close to the door, keeping a firm grip on Watson.

''No, thank you,'' I said, thinking regretfully of the fruitcake and tea I had left at home.

''It's my guess that the cat got into one of your cars when it was parked near my client's house over in the Parkside area. Mavis Byrde, I believe you know her?'' He started at the name, but made no comment. I went on: ''Would you mind checking your records to see if you rented to anyone in that area during the past two weeks?''

''I don't have to check. I haven't rented to anyone over there in weeks. Most of my customers are business people, from downtown.''

Then it had to be Clyde's car that Meowzart had got into. I had been put off the track by Mavis's statement that he never visited her house because of his allergies. Maybe so, but perhaps his allergies hadn't been enough to keep him from visiting another house in the neighbourhood.

''How about yourself? Have you driven over there recently?''

''Never go near the place,'' he replied. He shuffled

some papers on his desk and avoided looking at me directly.

"But you told me yourself you had hopes of acquiring property in that area once the new highway goes through."

"Yes, but—"

"What about Mrs. Walker, the woman who lived next door to Mavis, who was killed recently? Did you ever visit her?"

Clyde was unable to hide his astonishment.

"Never met the woman."

"But aren't you her stepson?"

"Who told you that?"

"Is it true?"

"What is all this? I thought we were talking about a lost cat. You're confused, little lady."

Ignoring his aspersions, I let him continue under the impression that I was a muddle-headed nosey parker.

"Such a pity about the poor old lady, getting killed like that," I said. "The police still haven't found the murderer, you know. It certainly makes one concerned for one's safety knowing there's a killer on the loose. I understand the police are questioning everyone. Have they spoken to you?"

"The police already have my statement. I was with Mavis Byrde the night of the murder."

"So I heard."

"The woman was a witch. So's her daughter, that palmist who calls herself Estelle LaBelle. Cat killers, both of them."

So he knew about Estelle's relationship to Lizzie Walker. And he also knew they had nothing to do with dead cats.

"Didn't you start the rumours of witchcraft yourself, taking advantage of the unusual coyote activity to put the blame on Lizzie and Estelle?"

"Why would I do that?"

"Because you wanted the property for your business expansion. But Estelle will inherit the house. And if anything happens to her, her child will inherit."

I waited for that to sink in.

"Her child?" he blustered. "I didn't know about . . . What makes you think I have anything to do with any of this?"

"The photograph in Lizzie's house. I saw it when I discovered the body. An old picture, in a silver frame, of Lizzie and her husband, and their two small children. You and your stepsister, Mary—Estelle, as she now calls herself. An amazing resemblance between you and your father."

He took a step toward me. Watson growled a warning, and at that instant the telephone rang.

I took advantage of his momentary distraction and made a hasty exit.

"I bet that call was from Mavis," I said to Watson as we drove down to the corner, made a U-turn, doubled back across the street, and parked out of sight.

And waited.

26

Samhain

IN LESS THAN five minutes Clyde's car pulled out of his parking lot and headed toward Parkside.

"Just as I thought," I said to Watson. "He's going to Lizzie's to look for the photograph. He thinks he's going to take it, then he can make me out a liar, or at best confused, as I won't be able to show the police the resemblance between him and the man in the picture. You'll see."

Of course, that meant Clyde didn't know the photograph was already missing.

Watson, no doubt regretting leaving the comforts of home to come out on this wild and windy night, didn't seem able to work up too much enthusiasm for the escapade, and settled down on the backseat with a deep sigh.

The wind buffeted the wagon as we made our way across town to Parkside, keeping several cars between us and Clyde. I trusted that he would be too absorbed in trying to avoid the last of the ghosts and goblins darting across the street to notice that he was being followed.

As the evening progressed the trick-or-treaters were older. When we passed the high school I had to stop at the crosswalk for a bunch of costumed teens going home from a football game—or, perhaps, on to a party.

I wasn't concerned about losing sight of Clyde. I knew where he was headed.

I turned off at the corner before Lizzie Walker's street and parked. Watson and I would cover the remaining distance on foot. As we rounded the corner I saw that Clyde had parked on the side street alongside Lizzie's house, taking advantage of some overgrown bushes so there would be less chance of his being observed. Though with everything else going on that night—the wind and the trick-or-treating—it was not likely that he would attract attention.

So it was that, approaching the house from different directions, we were both in for a surprise.

By the flickering light of a bonfire in Lizzie's front yard, a tall willowy figure was throwing something into the flames.

Someone else was helping her. The hood of his sweatshirt pulled up to protect him from the wind, Slippery Sam was piling kindling onto the bonfire.

Mavis came rushing out of her house.

''She'll have us all in ashes,'' she cried, her long blonde hair blowing wildly as she came over to the picket fence. Then, raising her voice so as to be heard above the wind, she shouted, ''I've already called the fire department and the police. What does she think she's doing?''

"Why don't we ask her?" I said. But Mavis, her face pale in the light of the flames, held back, staying on her side of the fence.

With Watson by my side, I advanced toward Estelle, uncertain of what to say, certain only of the need to reach her, to persuade her to dowse the fire before any damage was done. As I approached I noticed something gleaming in the fire's embers. It was Lizzie's photograph. Evidence was burning before my eyes. But any hope I might have had of retrieving it was thwarted by the impossibility of getting close enough to the red-hot coals against which the frame rested.

Estelle didn't appear to notice me at first. She seemed to be in a trance, mumbling incoherently while rocking over a cluster of small white stones that she held cupped in her hands against her body. Each had some kind of marking on it. Names, probably, I thought, remembering what she had told me. Names of loved ones—her daughter's, her son-in-law's, her granddaughter's.

What had she called Halloween? Samhain, or "summer's end." She'd said if any marked white stone could not be found among the ashes the next day, it was feared that its thrower would die during the coming year. Was Estelle trying to foresee her chances of getting through the coming year alive? Why would she doubt it?

In any event, there could be no doubt of the recklessness of lighting a bonfire on a windy night in a yard full of tinder-dry weeds.

The smell of smoke filled my nostrils, and I had to

brush sparks from my clothing. I tugged on Watson's leash to pull her away.

''Here,'' Estelle said, as if suddenly aware of my presence. ''Here is your stone. Throw it in when you're ready, and remember to come back and look for it on the morrow.''

On the morrow? She was certainly entering into the spirit of the occasion. Even her language had taken on a mystic quality.

I took the small white round stone from her hand, uncertain whether or not to comply. I wasn't immune to superstitions, having had many handed down to me from my British forebears—throwing spilled salt over one's shoulder, not picking up a dropped glove, not opening an umbrella in the house—many of which seemed to me to be based on mere common sense. But this particular belief was entirely too irrational for my taste.

''Do it,'' Estelle urged, her narrow face sinister in the firelight. ''It is bad luck not to cast the stone, once the name is down.''

Thinking it best to pacify her, I was about to toss the stone into the fire when my arm was caught from behind.

''Mrs. Doolittle.'' Detective Mallory's voice, though stern, was tinged with amusement. ''What are you doing?'' It was more a protest than a query.

''What does it look like? I'm celebrating Samhain,'' I said, not without a little bravado.

I became aware that others had arrived. Officer Offley's bulk loomed close behind Mallory; other police officers also. And there was Tony. How did he get there?

He went up to Sam and appeared to be arguing with him, trying to pull him away from the fire.

"Come on, mate. Let's get out of here," I thought I heard him say.

From the corner of my eye, I caught sight of Clyde about to enter the house through a side door.

Estelle had also seen him. "There he is," she cried, pointing a long, bony finger in Clyde's direction. "There's the man who killed my mother. And tried to trick her out of her home."

At that moment everything rearranged itself in my head. Clyde tried to trick Estelle's mother out of her home? How would she know that unless her mother had told her? If Clyde had killed Lizzie that night, the old lady would never have had the chance to tell Estelle.

With a nod of his head, Mallory dispatched Offley to apprehend Clyde.

The detective then turned to Estelle. "Ms. Walker, I am going to have to ask you to come down to the station for questioning."

With a cry of despair, Estelle threw the remaining stones into the flames all at once. "It was an accident," she moaned, her hands falling to her side.

Suddenly our attention was diverted by a scream from Mavis, still in her own front yard.

"The house! Look at the house! It's on fire!"

27

Watson to the Rescue

WIND-BORNE SPARKS FROM the bonfire had torched the tall cypress trees surrounding the house; from there the flames ignited the dry wooden shutters and sucked at the cedar-shake roof.

Neighbours from across the street raced to help. One grabbed a garden hose while another kicked open the front door, causing the fire to surge outside and return again to lash at the trees dotting the front yard.

"Oh, the rosebush," I cried at one point as the decades-old rambler I had admired a few days earlier was reduced to ashes.

Smoke and sparks drifted toward Mavis's house, where neighbours were busy dousing her roof and the fence.

The wail of approaching fire trucks could be heard above the sound of the wind and the crackling of the fire. But there was little hope of saving the house. The newspapers piled in the hall, the rubbish and the card-board boxes stacked in every available nook and crevice, had been biding their time for just such an event. The thought of the cardboard boxes led my mind to the Siamese mother cat and her kittens still, as far as I knew, in the kitchen.

"Watson, stay," I commanded her as she made to follow me.

Tripping over the yellow police tape now lying useless on the ground, I raced down the side yard and entered the house by the door through which Offley and Clyde had disappeared a short time earlier. Smoke filled my lungs and I snatched off my head scarf and pulled it around my mouth. Opening the kitchen door, I fumbled for the light switch, thankful that the electricity was thus far still working. The Siamese cat was pacing frantically back and forth, a kitten dangling from her mouth. I picked them up and dumped them into the box with the other two kittens, thinking as I did so, Only three? There were four kittens, I know there were four.

Tony and Mallory were on their way in as I stumbled out the door. Tony took the box from me while, coughing and staggering, I allowed Mallory to assist me through the smoke to the comparative safety of the front yard.

A firefighter came forward with an oxygen mask, but I pushed it aside. "I have to go back. There's another kitten in there," I gasped.

"The hell you do," said Mallory.

I knew he was right. I was weak from my exertions, my lungs were burning, my strength failing. Common sense told me I would be crazy to risk my life for a kitten. But sometimes common sense makes no sense at all.

The firefighter turned from me to the mother cat, now lying inert by her babies, and placed the oxygen mask over her face. After a few minutes she came 'round. Her fur was singed, whiskers gone. But she would survive.

"Are you all right?" Detective Mallory asked me.

"No, I'm cross," I answered irritably. "You kept me from going back for the other kitten—"

This exchange was mercifully cut short by a shout from Tony.

"Not to worry, luv. Look 'ere."

I looked up to see Watson coming down the side of the house carrying something in her mouth. She lay down and gently released the fourth kitten at my feet.

"Oh, Watson. Good girl. Naughty girl," I said fondly, stroking her head. By disobeying my command to stay, she had saved the kitten's life. I placed the tiny scrap of grey-and-white fur in the box with its mother.

While some firefighters poured water into the house and over the trees, others searched indoors for Clyde and Offley. They found them trapped upstairs in the turret room where the flames had started to penetrate. They suffered minor burns and smoke inhalation, but otherwise were unharmed.

It took less than thirty minutes to bring the fire under control, but when it was all over, only the brick chimney was still standing.

28

The End of the Affair

"BUT WHAT MADE you twig to the fact that Mavis was lying?" asked Tony.

We were on our way back to my house. Tony was driving. I was just too done in to be safe behind the wheel. In my embarrassment at having spoken to Mallory so sharply, I had refused his offer of a ride to the hospital emergency room.

The Siamese cat and her kittens were another matter. I had dropped them off at the all-night emergency animal clinic, promising to check on them in the morning. My answering machine had yielded a home for one of the kittens, I thought, recalling the man who had called on behalf of his mom. I might keep the mother cat and what I was already thinking of as "Watson's kitten." It was quite likely Evie could be persuaded to take another, perhaps even two. In any case, I was sure that, after the story of Watson's heroics appeared in the *Times* the following morning, there would be no shortage of offers of homes.

"It was the wind. The way it's been carrying the

sound lately,'' I said, answering Tony's question. "I didn't think much about it at first, but it kept cropping up. Like when Mavis said she heard voices arguing the night of the murder, but the next day when I went over to Lizzie's house to look for Meowzart, I heard the piano lesson. The wind was blowing in the opposite direction to what it would have been for Mavis to hear arguing.''

''But the wind direction could have changed,'' said Tony.

''Of course, and I wouldn't have thought any more about it, except that it's been so noticeable lately. The lifeguard on the pier, the high-school band practice. I checked the weather reports in back issues of the newspaper. For the past two weeks the prevailing wind has been fairly consistent.''

''She's right, you know,'' kidded Tony to Watson as we walked up the driveway to my house, to an excited yapping greeting from Trixie.

''What the 'ell,'' said Tony as the terrier, costumed as an angel, staggered toward him, wanting to leap into his arms as usual but hampered by the halo falling down over her nose and the wings slipping under her stomach.

Chamois, incongruous as a pink-faced devil, horns strapped tightly around his head and a red cape covering his back, stood uncertainly in the background.

Fortunately Watson had been spared such indignities—until now.

''Here, Watson,'' said Evie, coming forward with a witch's hat and perching it on the Dobie's head. Turning to me, she said, ''Did you remember my ciggies?''

I shook my head apologetically.

"Where have you been all this time?" she continued. "I have been quite run off my feet with trick-or-treaters. We ran out of sweeties hours ago, and I've been handing out money ever since. Fortunately I had quite a bit of change in my handbag. I'd been saving it for the next time we go to Estelle's." She made a circling motion over her hand. " 'Cross my palm with silver,' and all that."

"I'm afraid Estelle's fortune-telling days are over," I said, going on to explain to an astonished Evie the events of the evening.

Her eyes widened when she heard about the cat rescue. "I thought you looked a bit sooty," she said. "And my scarf, it looks like you wiped the floor with it."

"I'm sorry. I'm sure it will wash up quite nicely," I said, though actually I was sure of no such thing.

Evie, who had busied herself making us a cup of tea while we talked, carried the tea tray into the sitting room.

"Poor Estelle," she said. "Though I'm sure she had a perfectly good reason for acting the way she did. Mothers can be extremely tiresome at times. But it's most inconvenient. I had been depending on her to find out what it is that's bothering Chamois."

"Don't you worry about that there dog," said Tony, pointing his thumb at the little Maltese, whose only concern at that particular moment appeared to be ridding himself of the offending devil costume, shaking, rolling over on his back, trying to rub it off. "He's a lot smarter than you think. There's nothing wrong with 'im that a good romp on the beach now and then wouldn't take care of.''

''So what was all that about dead cats and witchcraft then?'' asked Evie, eager for details.

''From what I can make out, Clyde has been trying to get Lizzie to sell him the property for months. When that didn't work, he attempted to discredit her, maybe get her institutionalized, by starting the rumours of witchcraft.''

''What did I tell you!'' exclaimed Evie triumphantly.

''What he didn't know,'' I continued, ''until it was too late to avoid being implicated in the murder, was that Estelle was on the scene, and had her own ax to grind with her mother.''

''Sounds like they was all at fault one way or another,'' said Tony. ''All of 'em was lying—Estelle, Mavis, Clyde, the lot—all lying except me mate, Slippery Sam.''

''Certainly there's enough blame to go around,'' I said. ''If Clyde hadn't acted the way he did, which convinced Estelle that Lizzie really was crazy, and pushed *her* to the end of her rope, then Lizzie would still be alive today.''

''Bit of a nutter, that Estelle,'' put in Tony. ''Takes after her mum.''

''Sort of chain reaction, then?'' said Evie, adjusting Chamois's horns.

''Perhaps in the first place it was simply, as Dr. Willie suggested, a case of a careless coyote happening to drop his feral or stray cat prey,'' I said. ''But then Clyde found the carcass and decided to exploit the situation.''

WE DIDN'T LEARN the details until much later, during the trial. Estelle, overwrought with the strain of leading a double life, was furious when she learned that Lizzie had changed her will, leaving the house to the Buttercup Cat Retirement Home.

Their arguments had escalated during the days leading up to the murder, as Mavis testified, culminating in a final row when Estelle killed her mother by striking a heavy blow with the candlestick, the one that was on the altar when I discovered the body. She had cleaned it off, replacing it very carefully into the exact outline of the dust marks. But it had been impossible to clean the wax candle properly, and it had only been a matter of time before the police forensics unit examined it and matched the fingerprints. She had lit the candle in a pathetic attempt to mislead the police about the time of death, should her first alibi—that she was at the mall and the cinema—have to give way to the second—that she was in Winona at the time of the murder.

Clyde, for his part, had visited Lizzie later that night, to try to persuade her to sell him the property. He had discovered the body and left. He was the anonymous tipster. He knew his relationship with Lizzie would come out eventually, and had persuaded Mavis to back up his alibi.

''And Mallory didn't help by continuing to believe Mavis. Didn't even check out the alibi until the end,'' I said indignantly when telling Evie about it later.

"Just goes to show you," my friend replied. "Men will believe anything if it's daft enough."

IT WAS A day or two later. Tony and Trixie were back in their trailer, Evie and Chamois had returned to San Diego, and I was feeling quite let down after all the excitement. I didn't even have any current cases to work on. The missing Boxer had found his own way home, his whereabouts unaccounted for until several months later when a family on the next block threatened a paternity suit after their champion Basset presented them with a litter of unmistakably Boxer-cross pups.

A nagging cough contributed to my malaise, and I regretted not taking Detective Mallory's advice and going to the emergency room the night of the fire.

Belatedly I took myself to St. Mary's ER, where the doctor informed me I was suffering from exhaustion. All I needed was rest. He also told me that since I was, technically, a victim of an incident involving a police investigation, it would be necessary for him to file a report with the authorities.

The following morning I was indulging myself with a nice cup of tea and a piece of Great-Aunt Nell's Dundee cake when there was a knock at the door. Watson, as usual, beat me to it.

Detective Mallory stood on the porch. He was carrying a bunch of yellow roses.